DISCARD

D0888059

By T. STYLES

TRUCE

THREE

THE SINS OF THE FATHER

T. STYLES

ARE YOU ON OUR EMAIL LIST?

SIGN UP ON OUR WEBSITE

www.thecartelpublications.com

OR TEXT THE WORD: CARTELBOOKS TO

22828

FOR PRIZES, CONTESTS, ETC.

Truce 3: Sins of The Fathers

WWW.THECARTELPUBLICATIONS.COM

By T. STYLES

5

TRUCE 3

SINS OF THE

FATHERS

By

T. STYLES

Library of Congress Control Number: 2021902142

ISBN 10: 1948373475
ISBN 13: 978-1948373470

Cover Design: Book Slut Girl
First Edition
Printed in the United States of America

WAR
Series
in Order

War

War 2: All Hell Breaks Loose

War 3: Land of The Lou's

War 4: Skull Island

War 5: Karma

War 6: Envy

War 7: Pink Cotton

Truce: A War Saga

Truce 2: The War of The Lou's

*An Ace and Walid Very, Very Bad
Christmas*

Truce 3: Sins of The Fathers

Truce 3: Sins of The Fathers

What Up Fam,

I hope and pray this message finds you and your families in good health and happiness. It's a New Year, we have a New President, a Black Female Vice President and I just want you to take a deep breath and exhale! I feel a shift coming and I know we will be just fine.

Now...TRUCE 3...I just have to take this time to say I ABSOLUTELY love this saga! T. Styles is a wizard with how she created a world around the Wales and Louisville's and I am all in! With every new edition to this series, I fall more and more in love and TRUCE 3 did not disappoint! You WILL be dropping your jaws a few times while reading this I guarantee it!

With that being said, keeping in line with tradition, we want to give respect to a vet or new trailblazer paving the way. In this novel, we would like to recognize:

Kamala D. Harris

Madame Vice President Kamal D. Harris is a former US Senator, District Attorney of San Francisco, California Attorney General and has had a lifetime of public service. She is a member of Alpha Kappa Alpha Sorority, Inc. and a graduate of HBCU Howard U. I simply had to recognize Madame Vice President in this novel. VP to VP, we are extremely proud of Kamala and love the representation of the BLACK GIRL MAGIC we now have in the White House.

Ok, ya'll, get to it!
Love you!!
God Bless!

Charisse "C. Wash" Washington
Vice President
The Cartel Publications
www.thecartelpublications.com
www.facebook.com/publishercwash
Instagram: publishercwash
www.twitter.com/cartelbooks
www.facebook.com/cartelpublications
Follow us on Instagram: Cartelpublications
#CartelPublications
#UrbanFiction

#PrayForCece
#KamalaHarris

#TRUCE3

This story picks up where
AN ACE AND WALID, VERY,
VERY BAD CHRISTMAS
leaves off.

You Must Read That Book First

PROLOGUE

The earth against Mason Louisville's belly was damp and smelled of the foulness given to the air, when something living died.

And yet there he lie, on the ground, afraid that after everything he had done in life, some good, more bad, this would be his final moment on earth.

So, he took in what would inevitably be his coffin.

The coolness of the air.

The thump of his heart.

And the silent breathing of a predator who was nearby.

Before long, he could hear footsteps in the distance, and still, if he planned correctly, maybe the grim reaper would not find him. Besides, he was well hidden. And only the most vicious of snipers or hired killers would have thought to look for him beneath the house.

He could stay there in perfect darkness all night if need be.

And then something happened.

Something that on the scale of things, may not have seemed so bad.

Due to a few kicks of his boot, he had unraveled a bed of red fire ants, which took to crawling up his legs, and gnawing at the flesh of his ankles. To say it was painful was an understatement. Their tiny bodies worked diligently up his thighs, moving viciously toward his crotch area.

As if their primary focus was to get him to give up his position.

And yet, he had to take the pain.

He had to take the heat.

For if he did not, the agony of bullets would far outweigh the sting of their bites.

And so, he remained, hoping Mrs. Death would be denied, and pass him over once more.

CHAPTER ONE

THE PETIT ESTATE

JANUARY

Banks sat within the darkness of his bedroom. The window was open, and the moonlight greeted his handsome face. The way the stars lit up the Wales medallion that sat against his chest was so fucking sinful.

His silhouette had definitely changed since he started testosterone therapy back, and so his feminine features were a thing of the past. No one would have known about that dark period in his life.

No one would have known that the man before them was once Blaire Petit.

But he did.

With his silk black pajama shirt hanging open, revealing his new tattoos, he sighed deeply. So much had to be done, with so little time.

When his thoughts took a turn on the dark side, Jersey switched inside, wearing a red silk nightgown that raped the curves of her body.

The moment he saw her physique, he wanted to go deep between those thighs. To smell, fuck and taste her flesh.

Banks may have alternated his mood toward her when the sun shined on the land, when memories of her betrayal took hostage of his thoughts, but at night he was always in the mood for some pussy.

Walking over to him, she straddled him, while looking down into his eyes. The stars giving her frame a soft glow. "Blakeslee's asleep. And Walid gets dropped off tomorrow."

He nodded.

"What's good, nigga?" She dropped her box closer toward his spot, so he could feel her warmth.

He chuckled once. "What's up, sexy?"

"A wet pussy for your thoughts." She licked her lips and the bottom one sparkled.

He grinned. "Oh yeah?"

She grew slightly serious. "What you thinking?"

He sighed and decided to keep it real. "About time wasted." He grabbed her ass cheeks and squeezed. "About how I could've been back to myself years ago, had I known who I really was."

She ran her fingers through his short curly hair and scratched his scalp, knowing he loved the sensation of her nails. "Let the past stay the past, Mr. Wales."

"Oh yeah. Maybe you can help me with that."

She kissed him softly. "Maybe…" a wet kiss. "I…" a wet kiss. "Can."

In the mood to fuck, he nodded and then snaked his finger into her pussy. Dropping her head back, she

Truce 3: Sins of The Fathers

moaned at his touch. Before long due to his piano finger game, her clit was so oily, he could barely stay on the button without slipping off.

"You strapped?" She asked.

"I haven't taken it off since you gave it to me."

"It was always yours," she eased up a little and placed it inside of her body. "I just reminded you of your stroke game, that's all."

Once inside of her wetness, Banks positioned her hips for the taking. Their bodies swayed in a wave like motion, as if preparing for a storm.

Removing her breast from her gown, he suckled her nipple until it grew slightly between his lips.

She always smelled sweet.

Like expensive cologne and pineapple.

Picking her up, he laid her on the floor and pushed into her deeper.

Ah…

That was it.

With the top of the strap pressing firmly against Banks' spot, he was able to journey even further into her walls.

And Jersey, loving the sensation, wrapped her legs around his waist and pulled him toward her just a little bit closer. Fire roared between their flesh as her breasts smashed against his chest. Their skin connected in a way that couldn't be described.

So why bother?

The way she moaned...

The way she smelled, made Banks weak.

He could feel her juices dampening the strap and knew he would have to buy another one. But it was nothing.

Rich niggas do what rich niggas must.

"I love you, Banks." She moaned, while looking into his eyes.

He kissed her neck and sucked hard, making his mark for the world to see.

"I know you do."

Raising his ass high, he pounded rougher and rougher until he came so hard, she had to follow suit.

To Jersey, there was no sexier sound in the world than making a mean, billionaire ass nigga moan, so Banks gave her exactly what she needed.

Suddenly, all was good.

For now.

CHILDREN'S HOSPITAL

It was cold as fuck outside.

The forecaster lied and Mason was angry.

When he looked at the news earlier that morning, the weatherman said it would be cool and comfortable. Higher than 57 if he quoted him directly. And yet there he was, standing outside of the hospital, in a 20-degree storm, where his son Ace was being held, getting feathered with snow as he tried to keep his cigarette dry.

Mason Louisville was definitely on edge.

Not just because of Ace.

He also felt that at some point in January he would die.

He felt more certain than anything he ever felt before, and so, he wanted to make every second count. Starting with getting his son out of the facility which held him due to a manipulated mental breakdown from a grown ass woman.

Carmen Petit is what they called her.

He was getting another pull, when his phone rang. Removing it from the pocket of his chocolate fur lined leather coat, he dropped his cigarette and stomped out its flames with his Nike boot.

Dipping back into the warmth of the hospital, he answered.

But who was hitting him up?

He didn't recognize the number.

"Who this?"

He stepped out of the path of a woman who was stomping his way, with a stiff cough he wasn't feeling.

When the person on the other end didn't respond, he frowned and looked at the screen again. "I said who the fuck is this?"

Heavy breathing vibrated through the handset, sending chills down his spine. And suddenly the call ended, just as Banks strutted inside with Jersey at his right. He didn't know if he had gotten his memory back, but he could tell that the beat of his drum had changed.

Blaire was gone.

And a man was in her place.

He was wearing a black long peacoat with a fur lapel and a diamond that sat in his left ear that sparkled so hard, it looked like a wet icicle. His hair was back short, cropped and healthy. And his eyes were shielded with ombre smoked shades.

Of course, Jersey matched his steeze with a camel color peacoat over her leather catsuit and high red boots.

They looked like stars.

All of them were stars.

"Are they ready for us yet?" Banks asked, as his hands dipped into his pockets, as Jersey looped her arm through his.

Mason was going to speak to his ex-wife, but after Banks put him in his place the last time, they all met at the hospital, and he saw the hickey on her neck that enraged him, he decided they could both suck his dick.

"Not yet. The doctor was held up with another appointment." Mason sighed and looked at her briefly, before focusing back on his old friend. "You sure your girl should be here?"

Banks smirked. "You jealous or something?"

"Come on, son, you know it ain't about that shit." He swiped at the air. "But with everything going on, we should put on the best faces for Ace's doc. And the three of us sitting in front of him, to me, ain't it."

"Oh, so now you wanna put on the best faces?" Banks chuckled once.

"That's what I said."

"I'm not even surprised, you were always one for wanting to change how a nigga looks, huh?" That was a direct jab at Mason wanting him to be Blaire for his own sexual desires to hear Banks tell the tale.

Mason shifted a little, hands stuffed deeper in his pockets. "You know what I mean. I'm trying to get Ace back home. And this here, is too much." He looked at Jersey and glared.

"Let me be clear." He clapped once.

"You know what—."

"As long as I'm here, she's gonna be here too." He nodded her way. "If you gotta problem with that, then bounce. You ain't got no point here anyway." He nodded at Jersey. "Ace is our son."

"You see, that's where you wrong."

"Mr. Louisville," a young white woman wearing a pink glittered mask said walking up to them. A manilla folder was nestled closely to her chest. "Come with me. And do you all have masks?"

They nodded and quickly removed them from their pockets, covering their nostrils and mouths in the process. Normally they would be ready, but the three agitated each other so much they almost caught COVID off some dumb shit.

A few minutes later, they were inside a spacious office with so many professional degrees on the wall, it looked as if they were in an art museum for diplomas. Taking their seats in front of the desk, Jersey in the middle, the fellas on the outside, they waited for the doc to arrive.

"You can put your coats on the hook behind you if you'd like," Glitter Mask mumbled. They all looked at her and nodded as she walked out.

To be honest they wanted her gone.

They wanted everybody gone.

Especially each other.

For five minutes only the sounds of their breath could be heard within the room. And when Mason looked over at Banks, he was shocked to see him staring in his direction.

As if he wanted to take his life.

Although Banks eventually removed his gaze, if looks could kill Mason would be assassinated.

At that moment Mason wondered, was Banks the one planning to take his life? Was he the reason he couldn't get sleep at night?

Nah.

He don't hate me that much, he thought.

"Sorry to keep you waiting," A tall white doctor with piercing blue eyes said entering the room. He was wearing an KN95 mask with another over it which was the equivalent of putting the jimmy on extra tight.

After taking a seat behind his desk he sighed. "My name is Dr. Tony Porter, I'm your son's new doctor. And I want you to understand that Ace's care is my sole responsibility. So, now is the perfect time to —."

"What's going on with our son?" Banks asked, getting straight to the mothafucking point. He leaned in. "And when can we take him home?"

"It's easier said than —."

"It's a simple question. I mean, should we be worried or not?" Jersey added. "Because he's been here for weeks and I'm sure he's eager to get in his own bed, around his own things."

The doctor's eyes lowered. "I'm sorry to be so casual in my response. I deal with troubled children so much, that I can come across as cold at times. So how about we

Truce 3: Sins of The Fathers

do this…tell me who you all are, and how you relate to Ace, and I'll get straight to the point with our care plan."

Mason nodded his head. "My name is Mason Louisville, and I'm his father."

Banks frowned. "But you not though." He dragged a hand down his face. Focusing on the doctor he said, "My name is Banks Wales and *I'm* Ace's father."

"Banks, you and I both know I'm the boy's father. Why confuse the man? This is what I was trying to talk to you about in the lobby, son. But you were on a weird flex." He pointed at the door with his thumb.

"You not his father," Jersey said. "But I'm his mother."

Now Mason had lost reason. "Bitch, you will never be his mother in a — ."

Suddenly Banks flew out of the chair, in preparation to knock Mason out of his seat, until Jersey mixed into the situation by grabbing Banks' wrist, halting his moves.

And as Mason looked into his old friend's eyes, he could see the rage had nothing to do with Jersey. Banks was hurt by what he'd done, by denying him the truth of his past, and that alone made him sick.

Because when it was all said and done, he still cared greatly for the man known as Banks Wales.

"Listen, I don't know what's going on but if this is the kind of thing that has been happening around Ace, no wonder he is having a hard time." Dr. Porter said in a muffled voice under his mask.

Guilt dropped on all of their heads, as they reclaimed their seats.

"What I know to be true, is that if there are issues with the family, there will be issues with the children."

"We don't have issues," Mason shrugged, putting on a fake smile the man could see straight through.

"Something is going on. Now if we are going to get to the bottom of this, I need more information. Because based on what you all are saying, I'm definitely worried. And maybe, just maybe Ace is too."

THE LOUISVILLE ESTATE

Preach sat on Ace's bed, within the Louisville Mansion, talking to Walid who was sitting on his bed across the room. Since Christmas Eve, Walid was on edge. And it was obvious to all, that despite the very, very bad Christmas that took place in the house last month, that he missed his brother a lot.

"Son," Preach said softly.

"You not my father." He readjusted the diamond medallion on his rich ass baby neck.

"Huh?"

"You called me son and you are not my father."

Preach moved uneasily on Ace's bed. The kid spoke like he'd been here before, many, many times. He would need to talk as if he were a grown man if he wanted to get anywhere with him. "You're right."

"The name's Walid Wales."

Preach smiled. If nothing else the young king demanded respect, and so he had better give it to him. "Walid, did you notice anybody around this house, at any time when you were with your brother? On Christmas Eve."

He shrugged. "Anybody like who?"

"A woman. The woman Ace was telling us all about. The one who gave him the bow and arrow."

Walid frowned. "You weren't there."

"I don't get it."

"You said *us* and you weren't there. I don't remember seeing you."

Preach's original plan was to lie and say he was at the house on Christmas Eve. Especially since judging by

Truce 3: Sins of The Fathers

the story he heard, there were so many people present that the children were left unattended. And once again he learned he had better be careful, or risk losing the child's respect altogether.

"You're right. I wasn't there. But I still need your help. The woman who gave Ace the bow and arrow is dangerous. So, any information you can give me will be good, Walid."

Walid glared at him for a while.

A long while.

Finally, he said, "I don't like you. You're too jittery." He got up and walked away, leaving him alone.

When his brother left, Spacey entered the room and approached Preach. "Well? What happened?"

Preach sighed, rubbed his knees and stood up. "He doesn't know anything. I mean, if he does he's not telling me. The kid is intense."

"I told you he didn't know nothing in the first place. And I don't know where Carmen is, but you have to find out something. If Ace gets to come home, and that bitch is still roaming around, that could spell trouble for you."

"You threatening me?" He stepped closer.

Spacey matched his steps and moved two spaces in his direction.

"I know my father. Even with his memory loss, he won't tolerate someone fucking with his kids."

"His kids? He not even talking to ya'll niggas due to your disloyalty. If anything, me and Joey the only ones who were stand up when that shit went down with Mason. So, don't act like he cares about ya'll."

"I'm not talking about me, punk," Spacey attacked. "I'm talking about the twins. And don't worry, my father will forgive me. Because blood or not, I'm in his DNA. I'm in his bones. Now, if I were you," he pointed into his chest. "I'd put all my energy into finding Carmen. Because unlike me, his loyalty with you will die quickly. Trust."

RIVER'S APARTMENT

River, Mason's right hand Dom, was in bed looking up at the ceiling thinking about how different her life had been. At over six feet tall, with tats over every inch of her light skinned body, she looked like moving art.

She was smooth.

Suave.

And her masculinity got most women to look her way, even though some were straight.

The last few weeks with her ex-girlfriend Flower being back in her life was amazing. And at the same time, she got the impression that at some point things would change.

Call it intuition…

Call it anxiety…

Although she never admitted it to anyone aloud, she never got over being left by Flower after funding her dream to be a doctor. The pain was so great that at some points in her life she contemplated finding her and getting revenge, in the deadliest ways possible.

And yet here she was back in her life as if nothing changed.

The way Flower treated her, by leaving her for a man, whom she later married, after River paid for her education, was cold blooded.

And yet she couldn't resist her temptations.

Or maybe she didn't want to since she had time.

When Flower opened the bedroom door, holding a trey of bacon, eggs and sliced tomatoes seasoned with lemon pepper salt, River smiled. And since the window was open the sun bounced on it all.

Flower was wearing nothing but River's long white t-shirt which drowned out her frame, and a smile. The body bubbled in the meek fabric. River could still smell the scent of Flower's pussy on her lips and loved the fragrance.

"Breakfast for a king." Flower said before winking.

"You always talking shit."

"I'm serious." She sighed deeply and looked around the luxurious bedroom. "I knew you would do well for yourself but the life we have been living has blown me away. I feel like a star. You gotta have like what, half a million saved up?"

"More," River grinned.

Flower giggled. "So, what's the plan for today?" She handed her the plate of food and slid next to her in bed.

"Whatever you wanna do." She grabbed a piece of bacon and bit a chunk.

"You mean outside of fucking all day long?"

"You couldn't even take the dick a few minutes ago, and now you wanna go all day? Yeah, okay. Perfect your lane, shawty."

Flower rested her head on her arm thinking about her dildo game which was swift and good. When it came to sex, River was a master.

"I know I never said this, but I wanted to say thank you."

"For what?" River continued to eat her breakfast.

"For taking me back." She sat up and looked at her again. "When I called you on Christmas Eve, I wasn't sure if you would have me again. How I left was so fucked up but—."

"I really prefer if we don't bring up the past, Flower. It happened and I'm over it." She shrugged.

"Well, how come when I look at you, I still feel hate?"

River rolled her eyes and forked up her eggs. Why couldn't the girl let it go?

"Stop looking at a nigga then."

"River, if we gonna make it work, we have to be honest with one another. No games played. I can take it. And more than it all I deserve it."

"Like I said I'm —."

DING DONG!

Suddenly the doorbell rang within her large luxurious apartment overlooking downtown Baltimore. Confused on who was there, River eased out of bed and said, "I'll be back." Placing the food on the bed she moved toward the door.

"Don't make me wait too long." Flower winked.

DING DONG.

A little quicker now, River slipped into her plaid designer robe and shuffled to the door in her LV slippers. When she pulled it open, she was surprised to see Tinsley, her good friend, and the one person she missed beyond all standing, on the other side.

It was a shame they were beefing.

She loved him.

And he adored her.

"Hey, River."

"Tinsley," she nodded.

He looked sad but there was still the light behind his eyes she grew accustomed to seeing. And she wondered what was on his mind. And if he thought about her as much as she thought about him in the quiet moments of the day.

"Did I come at the wrong time?"

"You mean do I got a problem with you popping up without an invite? If so, the answer is yes."

Tinsley was a small, short man who could move between male and female so easily that River felt he was blessed with a gift. Although he was normally a feminine male, when he wore female clothing you would not be able to tell him from the real thing.

He was just that dainty.

He was just that beautiful.

"What you doing here?" River continued.

Truce 3: Sins of The Fathers

"I miss you." He folded his arms over his chest.

"You told me that multiple times already. But if you felt that you would've trusted me when I said I wouldn't let Mason hurt you, instead of running off with Banks Wales."

He looked down. "River, it's a new year. How long we gonna do this to one another? I never had a friend like you. I never had someone take care of me the way you did. All I want is for us to start all over."

River folded her arms across her chest. "So once again it's about you."

"I never said that. I'm just here being honest because I want to move forward with —."

"River, who is he?" Flower asked walking up behind her. She looped her arm through River's and pulled her closely to her side, as if she were real estate property.

"Go back to the room, Flower."

Flower didn't budge.

Tinsley frowned and then focused back on River. "Flower? Your ex-girlfriend!"

River looked away in shame and embarrassment.

"Please tell me you didn't take her back after what she did to you, River. This bitch is a fucking mess! A snake!"

"Excuse me!" Flower yelled, unlinking her arm from River's.

"You hurt my friend, whore!" Tinsley spit. "You ruined her life. And you were the reason me and Mason had to repair not only her mind but her heart. And now you wanna come back and reap the benefits?"

Flower looked at River to come to the rescue but was short. She had to defend herself in these streets.

"Oh, I get it!" She pointed at Tinsley. "You think you can fuck her because she moves and looks like a nigga. But let me be clear, you do know she's a lesbian right?"

Both River and Tinsley were put off by her comment. Up until that point no one publicly stated that the two were anything more than friends.

Because they weren't.

"Tinsley, I'm in the middle of breakfast. I can't do this with you now," River said. "Or ever to be honest. Don't come back here again."

"River, don't do this. I'm—."

"Go!"

Tinsley looked as if he had been ripped out from the inside. "Okay, I, I understand. But I'll call you later. All I ask is that you answer the phone, River. Please."

LOUISVILLE ESTATE

It may have been the morning, but Derrick and Shay were about to be on their midnight hour fuck shit.

As Derrick's dick swelled in his pajama's when Shay pushed her thick ass into him while they slept, he began kissing her on the neck. As he caressed her breasts and nipples until they thickened, he was ready to go all the way.

Pushing her on her back, as they lie in their king-sized bed, Derrick pulled off her pajamas, kissed in between her thighs and snaked his hands under her round ass cheeks. As he massaged them like dough, he began fingering her pussy while licking her clit like ice cream.

Morning head game was a glorious thing.

"Derrick, you feel so fucking good." She certainly applauded him for his efforts. "Damnnnn."

As Shay's screams grew more intense, Derrick knew that in a minute his work would be done.

"And you taste so fucking sweet," He managed to utter.

"Oh, Derrick what you doing to me?" She grabbed at the sheets. "I can't, I can't take no more."

Her words may have been saying one thing, but she continued to pump into his face at the same time.

Guess she could take it after all.

But Derrick didn't want her to bust just yet.

He made the pussy just right.

Shouldn't he get a chance to enjoy the fruits of his head game?

And so, after a few minutes of letting Shay get herself off, he rose, and pressed his throbbing dick sideways into her warm, wet center. His first few strokes were easy, but as her pussy became wetter and moister, his rhythm grew faster.

More intense.

He went to work.

Derrick, with his eyes closed, pounded Shay until she was drowning in her own juices.

Shay was at first speechless until she said, "Derrick, I love you. Please don't stop."

"Damn, your pussy wet as hell! How the fuck you get it like that all the time? Shitttttt!"

"Yes, baby! Can you please fuck me like this all night?" She really wanted to stay in bed and bone until the moon knocked on their home.

The answer was yes, but after a few more strokes, they both reached their tipping point, and the game was over.

Satisfied, Derrick rolled off her warm body.

Her breathing pattern slowed, as she relished the last few seconds of their explosive love making session.

"Why is it after all this time your pussy is still the bomb?" He grabbed a towel off the end table and wiped his dick half clean, which was softening.

"Because I let it marinate at night," she winked. "The way you like it."

He chuckled once and yawned. "Well, you deserve breakfast after that shit."

"I think Morgan comes back today from Christmas vacation."

"Nah, I'm cooking for mine." He eased out of bed. "Let me go make something for you and my son. It should be ready in twenty minutes." He moved toward the door. "Meet me in the kitchen."

"Derrick…"

He stopped and looked at her.

"I love you."

"I love you too, sexy."

When Derrick left the room, she rolled over on her back and looked up at the ceiling. She hated to believe it was true but for some reason after Ace's antics on Christmas Eve, the two of them seemed to be closer than ever. It was as if their marriage got revived. It was as if they got a second chance.

And she hoped it was true.

Even though she had suspicions that Derrick and Nasty Natty fucked at the Christmas Eve party. She had reasons to believe they went all the way. For starters she and Derrick fought and the next thing she knew, he was fixing his pants after being with Natty in the pool area alone.

Did they go all the way?

After getting Patrick ready for breakfast, she walked into the kitchen only to hear him talking.

Who was he speaking to so early?

When she approached him from behind, he quickly ended a call and plopped the cell phone in his pajama pants.

Shay felt as if she'd been dropped in an elevator shaft that wouldn't stop. He acted like he was hiding.

"Who, who were you just talking to on the phone?"

"Uh, nobody, bae."

It was Natty.

She felt it in her soul.

She dropped Patrick's little ass in his chair and stomped toward him where he stood in front of the stove. Her arms crossed her body tightly. "So, we're playing games now?"

"Shay, we just finished making love. Do you really want to ruin the day before it starts?"

In truth she didn't.

And at the same time, she realized something was slightly off. And yet, she couldn't say he was a bad husband. On the contrary, he was more attentive than he had ever been.

So why didn't she trust him?

She uncrossed her arms. "You're right, I'm tripping."

He walked up to her, snaked his hand behind her head and kissed her lips. She could smell her pussy in their kiss.

"Don't worry about it. I know things was shaky with us for a while. But we back. Let shit rock out. We got this."

Her eyes lit up. "You think so?"

He kissed her on the nose. Something he hadn't done before which was a weird flex.

"I know so, sexy. Now let me go shit. I'll be back to eat with you and Patrick. You can start without me."

As she walked to the table to prepare her and Patrick's plate, she noticed that Derrick was texting on his phone on the way to the back of the house.

Suddenly she didn't feel safe within their marriage anymore.

She didn't feel safe with Derrick having her heart.

Damn.

The romance was over.

SPACEY'S ESTATE

The sun shined through the soft yellow curtains in the kitchen as Spacey poured two cups of coffee. He and Lila just finished eating a heart sensitive breakfast and although the doctor warned her against caffeine, she begged him for a cup anyway just to steal a few sips of sweetness.

When he returned to the bedroom, he heard her talking on the phone. But she quickly stuffed it under her pillow as if someone gave a fuck.

Her weight had dropped considerably since she choked on a marble, and so the soft pink cotton nightgown that once held her 600-pound frame now played host to just about 500.

"You know you don't have to hide from me right?" Spacey said handing her the cup. "I don't care if you date."

"I know you don't. But I still don't think I should flaunt my relationship in front of you." She took a large sip.

Actually, she gulped it all in one breath.

"Like I said, it's not about that with me, Lila. I want you happy. And if he makes you happy that works for me." He sat in the recliner in their room and sipped his coffee as if he were her best good girlfriend who was trying to hook her up. "The only thing I'm concerned about is co-parenting. And if he's going to be a good man around my son. Because that's the only time I will flip."

"Spacey, he's a wonderful man. There's no need to threaten him."

Spacey sat his cup on the table. "You have to understand the difference between threatening and making a firm statement, ma. Our marriage was over a long time ago. And I'm good on that. But what I'm not okay with is a stranger being around my son with malice in his heart."

For a second she looked at him and glared. "You know what, you taking this really easy. All you seem to care about is Riot."

"I said I want you happy. So, it's obvious I care about you too."

"No, you don't." She pointed at him. "I believe in my heart your only concern is our son. Is that all you ever wanted from me? A child?"

He shrugged and thought about her question. "I don't know. And I don't wanna lie."

"Wow!"

"I know it's foul. And I'm sorry I came into your life at the wrong time. But the only thing that's important to me now is — ."

"Let me guess. Minnesota Wales."

"That's not fair."

"It's fair and true. You never cared about me really. But then again nobody in the Wales family gives a fuck about anybody but themselves. I don't know why I thought things should be different."

He could tell she wanted to fight. The thing was he didn't care to fight a situation that was done.

At the end of the day, he wanted out.

At the end of the day, he wanted his son happy.

And at the end of the day, he wanted his family repaired.

And Lila had no place in the new world order.

Period.

MINNESOTA'S ESTATE

As Minnesota sat across the dining room table from Zercy as he told a story she couldn't help but smile. The man was perfect in every way to hear her tell it and she couldn't believe that she was in a functional relationship for the first time in her life.

One that didn't compromise her mind, body, or soul.

Zercy for sure appeared to only want the best for her.

He appeared to only want to keep her safe.

And she adored him for it, especially since she didn't have a relationship with Banks anymore. Was it possible that her man, could raise her into a woman too?

"You are so silly," she said sipping her hot chocolate from a large red cup. "You know you didn't eat no ten hot dogs at once for no contest."

"And you are so beautiful." He sipped his coffee. "Even if you don't believe me. It's true by the way."

"Why do I feel sometimes as if I don't deserve you? As if everything we have together is all a dream."

Minnesota was tired of saying the same thing over and over to the man.

"You mean our world is a lie?"

"Yes."

He sat his cup down. "Get over here."

She walked toward him and sat on his lap. "What, boy?"

Rubbing her thigh, he said, "I prayed for you. I mean I really prayed for you, Minnie. So, you may not think you deserve me, but I deserve you and we will have a life that…"

Suddenly Minnesota's stomach began to churn.

Fearing she would throw up on him, she jumped up and rushed to the bathroom. Vomiting up everything she ate for breakfast she was hoping she didn't have some weird illness that was floating around.

Or could she be, well, pregnant?

The last time she was pregnant it was by Spacey and she wondered if it was possible for her body to go through bearing a child again.

KNOCK! KNOCK!

"Minnie, you okay in there?" Zercy asked banging on the bathroom door.

"I'm not sure, but I think I'm fine," she grinned. "I'll be out in a second."

CHAPTER TWO

CHILDREN'S HOSPITAL

The psychiatrist was definitely nervous…

The last time he had Banks and Mason in his office along with Jersey, things got heated and security got involved. And at the same time if they were going to go forward, and if he was going to return the child to their custody based on his assessment, he needed answers.

And he needed all parties calm.

"I'm hoping we can start over from scratch," Dr. Porter said.

Banks cleared his throat and rubbed his hand backwards through his curly hair. "So how long do we have to do these meetings and shit? I mean, I wanna see my son."

"What do you mean how long?"

"I think his question was simple enough." Jersey said crossing her legs. "How long do we have to come to these meetings before you release Ace to us? He already had Christmas in this facility. He also missed the New Year. How much more will he miss until you're satisfied?"

"To be honest I'm not concerned about holidays." He clasped his hands on his desk. "They're superficial anyway."

"What, nigga?" Mason glared. "Because that's not answering the question."

Doc was shook at his rage.

"The problem is I have yet to get the answers to any of my questions. And until I get to know those most involved in Ace's life, I don't know when I'll give my recommendations." He sat back in his chair. "So, let's start with what happened on Christmas Eve."

Mason sighed because they knew all in the room would blame him since he was in his custody. "To be honest everything went down so fast. We were having a party And Ace had a few of his cousins—."

"They aren't his cousins," Jersey interrupted, shaking her head. "Try and keep up, Mason. They are his siblings and nephew."

The psychiatrist shifted a little in his seat.

Mason wanted to smack her ass.

"I know this is uncomfortable but in order for me two understand the dynamic of this family and best serve Ace I need to know who each of you are," Dr. Porter said. "This time without fighting. And this time I ask that you talk directly to me."

Banks took a deep breath because it all felt like too much. "I'm not going to lie; I'm confused on a lot of this too."

"How so?"

"I suffered a brain injury some years back. And it caused me to forget things. But the heart of who I am has always been male."

"I'm still confused."

"Banks is trans," Mason interjected since they appeared to be beating around a dry ass bush. "Using his eggs, he mothered Minnesota Wales, Blakeslee Wales, via a surrogate, and the Twins. But also, while married to another woman, she had children for him. And they are Harris Wales, who passed away. Spacey, Joey and Shay Wales who he adopted after she lost her parents."

Jersey rolled her eyes at her ex-husband.

"When I had a brain injury Mason lied to me and told me we were married. And so, I lived as a woman for most of the twins' lives. I later found out who I really was and that everything he said to me in an effort to get some pussy was a lie. Because in actuality I had a whole life with Jersey."

The psychiatrist took a deep breath. "I believe I know what's going on with—."

"We're not done." Banks said. "I want to get all of this out in the open because I don't want to have to ever explain this to you again."

Dr. Porter nodded.

"And so, when I learned of Masons betrayal, I left home for a while. Maybe this is one of the reasons Ace acted out. And now all I want is to bring them back to live with me permanently."

Mason glared at him. "What does that mean? *Live with you permanently.*"

"It means that I and Jersey want to raise them in a loving—"

"If you're going to tell the doctor the story tell him the whole story," Mason interrupted. "Tell him how I was married to Jersey and you two fucked behind my back." He shook his head. "I may have lied, but you're not a martyr, Banks. I told you that before. I know you think you are, but you're as guilty as the rest of us. And if you think I will let you two bitch's raise my boys without me you don't know me at all."

"I don't want you anywhere around the twins," Banks said firmly. "You not hearing me! Ace cut up after leaving them with you. When they lived with me at my grandmother's estate there were never any problems. And now I haven't seen Ace in over a month. I put that on you." He pointed his way.

"What about the people in the attic!" Mason reminded him. "Because that sounds like a problem to me! Since you so perfect!"

Banks wanted him dead.

"Okay everyone calm down. This is not about custody right now." The doctor paused. "This is about —."

"I'm never going to be out of the picture, Banks. I need you to understand that. I don't know what you and my ex-wife have planned, but it doesn't matter. Because my other kids may have had rough roads, but I will see to it that—."

"Not rough roads," Jersey interrupted. "You destroyed our sons lives with your narcissism. And now one of my surviving children is missing and possibly dead." She was referring to Howard.

"As you can see it's two against me." He said to the doctor, hoping for some help.

He got none.

While they talked, Banks looked at Jersey and thought about the dream he had in which he witnessed Howard's murder. To this day he was certain that it was Mason himself who took his own son's life.

He had no idea, that it was he who gave the word for Howard's death.

"So, if you think being involved with the twins means what you did to our sons, then you can go fuck yourself."

Mason stood up almost knocking the chair behind him on the floor. "You know what, I done fucked both of these whores and I'm done with the disrespect. Don't even know why I'm listening."

"Mason, you about to make me—."

"What?" Mason said to Banks.

Banks smiled.

"Like I said, I'm not going anywhere," Mason continued. "But I'll show you better than I can tell you."

He charged out of the office.

HERCULES' HOUSE

While texting on the phone Natty exited her car and walked up to the expensive brownstone in downtown

DC. Tucking the cell in her pocket she ascended the large staircase and knocked.

Within seconds the door opened, and Hercules came outside. He was a tall man with greying hair and blue eyes, who still held onto his good looks despite his advancing old age.

Kissing her passionately, he grabbed her hand as they both disappeared into the house.

What neither of them knew was that Preach was sitting in his car not even a block down looking at them both with disdain in his eyes. Believing he was already onto something, he called Banks.

"Did you find Carmen?" Banks breathed into the phone. "I'm getting agitated at this point."

He moved uneasily in his driver's seat. "No, uh, not yet."

"Then why are you hitting my phone?"

He cleared his throat hating how after so long he had finally been able to reconnect with Banks only for him to look at him differently. Before Banks' brain injury, he and Preach were close. Just as close as Banks was to his father Rev. And now it was as if Banks didn't know him at all.

It was as if Preach was merely a set piece in his larger game to find the woman he believed was responsible for Ace's downfall.

The saddest part was that before Banks reemerged in his life, Preach was having hard times financially. He had a wife who despite her best efforts of going to the dollar store once a month, had expensive tastes. Tastes that Preach could not fulfill with being on the run, due to believing that Mason wanted him dead.

And as a result, they lived hand to foot.

Now that Banks was back in his life prosperity had returned. With the acquisition of Strong Curls, Banks was legitimately wealthy. He was also hood wealthy. Which meant his name still reigned in the streets and corporations around the world.

His presence was synonymous with bitcoin and coke money.

Even if he no longer indulged.

So, messing up at this time was simply not an option for Preach.

He had to find Carmen.

"I'm calling because I'm looking at Natty and I see her outside of your uncle's house kissing him. I don't know if you knew about their relationship so I'm checking in."

"Who is Natty again?"

"Oh, uh, she's Minnesota's friend. Well, she *was* Minnesota's friend. I'm not sure if they talk to each other now."

"Oh. I can't talk now. But what I want you to know is this, I need Carmen found. She's the reason I'm unable to have a relationship with my son. Do whatever you have to, to find her. And Preach, if you fuck up, you dead to me."

When Banks ended the call Preach felt gut punched.

Still, it couldn't be said enough that this was all Preach's fault.

After all, if he kept an eye on Carmen, Banks' aunt, when he kidnapped her before Banks' brain injury, she would never have gotten out and manipulated Ace into going crazy.

So, he had to right his wrongs.

His livelihood depended on it.

When Hercules brought Natty some tea per her request, he sat it on the table in front of her and plopped in the recliner where he could see her fully as she posted up on the couch while texting.

She had a new boyfriend he was certain.

The intense stare coming from his eyes put her on pause and so she tossed her phone to the side and folded her arms across her chest. "What is it, Hercules? I know that look."

"Are you drunk?" He crossed his legs, grown man style. Ankle to knee.

"I had a little something. Why?"

He glared and shook his head. "What is wrong with you? You told me you were pregnant and now you're drinking? Are you trying to kill our baby before it's even born?"

"Stop tripping! I have a grace period before I have to get all serious."

"A grace period?"

"Yeah, the baby is fine in the earlier days of my pregnancy."

"I'm sorry, how many babies have you birthed again?" He asked sarcastically. "Because I forgot."

"You know what I mean." Her left foot jiggled.

"Actually, I don't." He leaned forward. "But what I want you to understand is this, if my baby comes out with two dicks, I will blame you. I will also fight for custody and then blame you even more in court. And I'm old money, so I will win."

"Well, what about me blaming you? Because we should not have even been having sex since you kidnapped me. Remember? So, you ain't no poster father, whitey! Now I told you I will be a good mother. You just need to worry about Banks."

"There you go with the racist shit again." He shook his head. "And what about Banks?"

"How do you think he will act when he knows I'm pregnant with your child?"

Hercules smiled in a way that said he knew something everybody else didn't. "All Banks is worried about is finding Carmen due to whatever he thinks she did to Ace. Nothing less or more."

"Do you know where she is?"

"I haven't spoken to my sister in years." He scratched his forehead. "I told him that already."

"That makes you safe?"

"What I know about Banks is this, he places money in my account every month. A lot of money too. Some people may say it's not a big deal since my mother gave me a stipend before she died. But Banks, despite how much he disliked some of my actions took it upon himself to give me and my brother a little more. So, if you have a baby, and that baby is a part of the Petit bloodline, I think he'll bless us even further."

"So, hold up…you're doing this for money?"

"I never said that. I'm just stating that Banks is a good man. And good men look out for their families. Even if he's not feeling it. So, you take care of my baby by doing right by your body or you will see an evil side to me. Are we clear?"

THE PETIT ESTATE

Banks and Jersey walked through the doors of his large estate that was left to him in the will by his grandmother. He was angry about how things went at Dr. Porter's and at the same time he knew Mason would react exactly as he did, in an attempt to stay in their lives.

In an attempt to stay in *his* life.

"I'll go and make you some coffee," Jersey said as she kicked off her shoes and placed them by the door.

"I don't want coffee." He flopped back on the sofa.

"But you always take your coffee in the—."

"Be honest with me," he said seriously. "Do you think any of this, with Ace, is my fault?"

Jersey had to tread easily.

The last time she gave her opinion about the twins or Mason, Banks grew angry. Pushed plates off the table and everything.

Because at the end of the day he still wasn't sure if he could trust her, of this Jersey was certain.

After all, when Mason acted as if he and Banks were married, she was a part of Mason's supporting cast.

She sat next to him. "I think things will work out as they need to work out. They always do."

He glared. "That's not telling me anything. I'm asking you a fucking question! Talk to me." He slapped the back of his hand into his other.

"Banks, I don't feel comfortable giving my opinion with what's going on with you and Mason. Or the twins. But I will say that although Walid and Ace require your immediate attention, you have other children who you haven't spoken to since all of this kicked off. And if I could talk to Howard, Patrick or Arlyndo, just once, I would give anything to hear their voices."

"They betrayed me."

"They made a mistake. They were victims to a master manipulator, but they are still your children. And they need you."

"That's not fair." He wiped the air with a flat hand.

"Banks, whether you remember them or not, if something happens to them it will hurt. You don't know how badly I feel that I don't know where Howard is." She shook her head. "What I wouldn't give to have answers. What I wouldn't give to know if he's okay. I don't speak a lot about him, but his disappearance troubles me every fucking day. Do you really want that kind of guilt on your heart? Only because you refused to talk to your children."

"I'll take Tea. Not coffee."

She took that as a dismissal and bounced.

When Jersey left, Banks decided to see what Walid was up to as he was at the house now, after being dropped off earlier by the Louisville's.

And he wasn't looking forward to his attitude either.

Because every time Walid saw Banks, the confusion in his mind with him being male kicked up. It didn't help matters that he was back on hormone therapy in an effort to resume feeling like himself, so his temper was shorter.

Banks understood Walid.

He, himself was still confused.

Before Banks learned that everyone around him was lying, he was Blaire. When he returned as Banks his change although in line with who he really was, shocked Walid. To the point where he did not want to be bothered with him, if he wasn't dressed as his mother, something at the moment he wasn't willing to do.

Once at Walid's door, Banks opened it without knocking.

The Butler, Carl, was inside playing chess with him. He taught him how to play over the past weeks and as with everything, the boy picked it up quickly.

A baby genius if you're into labels.

"Leave us alone."

The Butler rose, his green eyes peering their way. He nodded and walked out the room.

"Are you getting any better?" Banks asked. "At the game."

Walid adjusted his diamond chain. His hair pulled back into a tight fluffy ponytail. "I don't feel like talking to you."

Banks wanted to snap. "I'm not taking the disrespect much longer, Walid. No matter how you feel, I'm still your parent."

"I want my mother. I don't want a parent. Where is she?"

"I'm right here. I never left you. "

"Yes you did! And I don't want to talk to you like this! I hate your stupid face! Where is your hair? Yuck!" He ran away.

Feeling defeated, Banks plopped on the bed and ran his hand back through his hair. At the same time Jersey entered holding two cups of coffee, not tea, because she knew that's what he preferred, no matter what he said.

She handed him a cup and sat next to him.

Taking a deep breath, she sighed. "Things will work out, Banks when you get everything in order. Work on what you can change right now and leave the rest alone. I know it seems bleak, but Walid will come around. You just have to give him some time."

"I hope you're right. 'Cause he for sure is not feeling me. And the shit hurts."

LOUISVILLE ESTATE

Shay and Derrick were getting dressed in their bedroom.

When he received a text message, her eyes, which were once on the brush in her hand and the bristles going through her hair quickly moved to his cell phone instead.

She knew in her soul he was on the phone with Natty.

And she felt it was half her fault, since she practically handed him over to her ass.

Derrick pressed a few buttons and drop the phone into his pocket. He didn't even look her way. Until recently he never took a call or responded to a text without at least telling her who was on the other line. But now he seemed to be in a world of his own.

A world that didn't include Shay Wales-Louisville.

"Are you going to tell me who that was or nah?"

He looked over at her. "Nah."

"Derrick is everything okay with us? Because at one point we seemed to be moving ahead in the next –."

"See, you wanna fight." He pointed at her. "And I've already explained to you I'm not gonna fight with you no more. Just because I don't tell you who's on my phone every five minutes doesn't mean there's an issue or another bitch. Chill! I made you my wife. That should be good enough."

"Congratulations to me, huh?" She frowned.

"What does that mean?"

"Whatever, Derrick. You gonna do what you want anyway."

"Exactly."

He shook his head and walked out the room leaving her stuck. She was about to make a decision whether or not to cry or to fight until she heard the doorbell ring.

Instead, she quickly got dressed, rushed out the room and looked at the video cameras. After verifying who was on the other side, she opened the door eager to get a mental escape.

Within seconds, River strutted inside with Flower on her arm. Shay hugged River having liked her, and having seen her on a regular, she also smiled at Flower.

"Hey, River. Mason not here yet."

"Yeah, I know. He just hit me and told me he was on his way though." She raised the liquor bottle in her hand. "I'm gonna pour out a little before he gets here since he not fucking with the alcohol no more. Is Derrick back there?"

"Yeah, he in the back."

She nodded and walked off leaving Shay with Flower.

"What's up with you? You look upset." Flower said rubbing her shoulder as if she knew her well enough.

Before she could respond Mason entered his house. His head was low, and his energy was dark. It was obvious that he wasn't in the mood to be chivalrous.

But Flower, in desperate need for Mason's approval since River liked him so much smiled brightly. "Hi, Mason! It's nice to see you again."

He glanced at her, shook his head and focused on Shay. After all, it was he who saved River's life when she tried to kill herself after Flower left her for a man.

"Tell River I'm in my lounge," he said to Shay, ignoring her all together once more.

Flower glared in his direction, as anger coursed through her veins. What she wasn't sure about but had an idea was that Mason didn't fuck with her.

At all.

And it was proven when he glanced at her again, shook his head and walked to the back of the house.

She was so embarrassed she looked away due to feeling uncomfortable. And then, suddenly, she smiled.

"Don't mind, Mason." Shay said waving the air. "He don't mean no harm."

"He do means harm. Still, I'm not tripping off of him, plus I know things." She continued to look in the direction he exited.

"You know things like what?"

"Girl, too much to tell right now." She batted her eyes. "After all, River shares everything with me." She paused. "But Shay, I know you don't trust me or even know me, but I'm more worried about you."

"I wouldn't say I don't trust you."

"It's cool if you don't though." She shrugged. "But I want to be a part of this family. You don't know how it feels to be an outsider. To be someone that everybody thinks about as an afterthought. Maybe we should stick together me and you."

Shay knew exactly how she was feeling. After all, she always felt like the black sheep with the Lou's and the Wales'. Maybe it wouldn't hurt to talk to her about Derrick.

Besides, what harm could come of confiding in River's girlfriend, since she was mostly family anyway?

"Okay, I think Derrick is cheating on me."

"Do you think or know?"

"I think. I mean, don't get me wrong, he hasn't been known to cheat but, I don't know, something feels off."

Flower stepped closer and looked behind her to be sure they were alone. "Maybe it's something else. Something he's keeping from you. Still, put your foot down, Shay. And if he fights, hit him where it hurts, no matter what that may mean for your marriage. He'll learn to respect you."

"Bae, I'm about to talk to Mason," River said walking into the foyer. "I be back."

"No rush, honey," Flower said smiling. "We just having girl talk. I'm good."

HERCULES' HOUSE

Preach waited all day for Natty to come out of Hercules' crib. He was tiring of feeling like a loser. And at the same time, he needed direction. Direction that Banks didn't seem to want to provide, and so when he saw his wife's number he quickly answered.

Maybe she would know what to say.

"Where are you?" She asked.

" I'm at work." He continued to focus on the house. "And shit is fucked because I don't know what to do next."

"Do whatever you have to protect our lifestyle. Do whatever you have to protect what we've built. Because I don't want to go back to living in motels, Preach. I don't wanna go back to not being able to eat where we want or go where we want. Go hard for our family. That's what you need to do."

He took a deep breath and sat deeper in his seat. "I know you're right. Don't worry, I won't let anybody take away what we have. I'll hit you soon."

Five minutes later another car pulled a few feet away from Preach's. The driver got out and quickly slipped into the passenger seat of his car. He was a tall yellow man with eyes so light brown they were almost see through.

They called him Michigan.

"Are you ready?" Preach asked.

"Whatever you need it's done." Michigan said.

"Good, when you see her snatch her ass."

"She won't know what hit her."

An hour later, Natty walked out of Hercules' house. Michigan, having been giving the game play, jumped out of the car and yanked her, while carrying her to Preach's ride.

She fought a few moments but eventually calmed down when she saw Preach's face. Perhaps this was just an interview and not a kidnapping.

"Preach, what's going on?" She asked while breathing heavily.

"Where's Carmen?"

"Carmen? How am I supposed to know?"

"Because you're the one who fucking her brother!"

"Preach, I don't know where she is. As a matter of fact, Hercules brought her up earlier and he doesn't know where she is either. Did you ask Banks?"

"I don't believe you." He glared at her, before scratching his head.

"I have to leave so I'm about to bounce. I'll holla at you—."

"I'm sorry, I don't believe I made myself clear. Bitch, you not going nowhere."

CHAPTER THREE

LOUISVILLE ESTATE

M ason was in the lounge within his mansion pacing next to the empty bar. Banks had irritated him at the doctor's and his temples throbbed. Although all of the alcohol had been removed since he had given it up, he still savored it to the day.

River, who had been waiting on him approached him inside. She washed her mouth down with Sprite to mask the smell of liquor so she wouldn't entice him. But ever since Tinsley showed up, she had been thinking about him and so she needed a swig or two throughout the day.

"Aye, Mason," she said shaking his hand and pulling him into a one arm hug. "Oh yeah, before I forget, the house lady asked to speak to you when I was on the way inside. What's her name again?"

"Morgan." Mason sighed deeply.

Although he respected her, and she was responsible for making him feel a little better when the secret of his betrayal against Blaire came out, she was the voice of reason. And he didn't want reason.

He needed rage.

"I'll get up with her later."

She walked deeper inside. "Are you okay?"

"Banks is trying to keep me away from the Twins. Can you believe that shit?"

"How is that possible?" She walked over to the bar, out of habit and picked up his phone.

Mason flopped on the sofa. "He thinks it's my fault that Ace acted out the way he did on Christmas Eve. When that couldn't be further from the truth. I love my boys. And would do nothing to hurt them."

"Can he really keep you away from them?"

"I don't know but I may have to get a lawyer."

She didn't like that shit one bit.

"I understand that you feel you have to get the law involved, but I don't know about all that. Banks is really fragile right now, considering how things went down. Maybe that's the wrong move."

"It's not the *law*. It's a *lawyer*. He wants to fight with me because of the Blaire shit, and so he keep the boys from me?" He put his hand over his heart. "When they got my blood? They ain't just cute cause of that nigga. They cute cause of me too!"

River wondered what cuteness had to do with anything.

"Nah, son," Mason continued. "There ain't shit in me that will allow that to happen."

River put his phone down, paced the floor and rubbed a hand down her jaw. She was desperately trying to fix her words before speaking. She decided to shoot straight from the hip.

"I don't know if you should challenge Banks."

Mason glared. "So, you saying he more powerful than me?"

"I'm not saying that he's more powerful. I'm saying he's angrier. That makes him more dangerous. The few times I dropped you off at the hospital and saw him walk in behind you, I saw the hate in his eyes. The person that you remember is no longer there. And challenging him in that way may not be worth it."

" I had four sons before the Twins and Bolt were born. And I destroyed their lives by not being a present father. I'm not gonna let them push me away from the Twins. Banks may be doing this because he's angry, but I can get mad too."

"I wanna be real with you."

"Of course."

"I think you may be doing this in an effort to hold on to Banks. And I want you to realize that it won't work this time. I'm begging you to be cautious. You're the closest thing I got to a father. And I don't want you to die simply because you aren't heeding my warning."

Mason would give anything for a glass of whiskey.

"I've known Banks all my life. We've been here before. And I can say with 100% certainty that he would never do anything to hurt me. Granted, I've thought about him being foul before, but our history is too deep. My only objective is to stay in the Twins lives. And I can't risk something tearing us apart."

River heard him but she was standing her ground.

To her, pursuing the Twins wasn't a good look. And she would do all she could to get through to him even if he didn't want to hear what she had to say.

At the end of the day, she would protect him at all costs.

Or die trying.

SPACEY'S ESTATE

Spacey was in the house getting ready to put Riot in bed to take a nap. Instead of doing everything on his own this time, he hired help.

"I'm about to go take a jog," Spacey said to his assistant grabbing his water bottle. "Keep an eye on Riot while I'm out."

"Yes, sir."

"Lila may check on him too, but I shouldn't be gone long. I doubt she'll leave the room though. But after that, I'm going to see about my little brother Walid. He hit my phone."

"Before you leave, sir, there was somebody hanging around the house. I don't know who they were, but I figure you may want to know."

"Were they male or female?" He frowned.

"I can't say. They were sitting in a black car with tinted windows. Again, it could be nothing. But I know there aren't any other houses near you. And figured if they were sitting on the block then they were here for some reason."

Spacey was definitely on edge. But he made mental notes to increase security until he found out what was going on.

MINNESOTA'S ESTATE

After taking a test, Minnesota was certain that she was pregnant.

Although she didn't intend to get in the family way again, after being pregnant by Spacey, she was happy Zercy was the father.

But would he be pleased?

Or would he think it was too soon to make a family?

He was sitting in their bedroom on the recliner reading when she walked in with a look on her face that put him on pause. Closing his book, he said, "Are you well? I've been worried about you all day."

"I have to talk to you about something." She sat on the side of the bed.

He sat up straight. "You can talk to me about anything. You know that."

"I hope that's true."

"Before we go any further, I want to ask you something." He reached into his pocket and pulled out a small burgundy ring box with gold trimming.

Her eyes widened. "Please don't scare me. "

"The last thing I wanna do is scare you, baby. What I want is for you to be my wife." He slipped out of bed, dropped on one knee and flipped open the lid.

Standing before her was a ring staring at her as large as a human eyeball. She trembled. "Zercy, see I have to talk to you first. More than ever."

"Right now, I need to know if you're gonna make me the happiest man on earth. Anything else is everything else." He held her hand. "Nothing is more important than this moment right now. Will you be my wife?"

She decided to be straight up instead of beating around the Bush. "I'm pregnant!"

The smile on his face put all of her fears at bay. She'd seen him light up in the past when he looked at her. But the expression on his face after having learned that he would be a father topped them all.

"Minnesota, I didn't think you could make me happier. I was wrong. Being your husband and raising our child together will be the highlight of my life." He softly squeezed her hand and pulled her towards him. "Now, would you do me the honor of being my wife?"

"Yes, baby, yes!"

They kissed and embraced for what seemed like forever.

When they separated, she paced around the room excitedly. Her mind was moving all over the place.

Would it be possible that the marriage to a man she had fallen hard for in such a short period of time could be the reason the family comes together again?

"I want to tell everyone. About our wedding. Or engagement."

"You can tell them whatever you want!" He pulled her closer and planted a kiss on her lips. "Just as long as by sometime next year you're my wife."

Minnesota didn't want to wait to break the news to her family.

She decided to bring everyone together.

Even her brother Spacey.

PETIT ESTATE

Banks was preparing to take a nap after the long day. And for some reason what Jersey said about his adult children played on his heart. Prior to her mentioning them, he felt a longing, like something was missing and now he wondered if their absence was what plagued him.

Although angry with Minnesota , Spacey and Shay all at once, he realized it was time to move on.

It was time to forgive.

How could he call himself a good parent if he isolated his children over a mistake?

He was just about to get some rest when his cell rang. Thinking it was Preach, he answered without looking at the number. "You find her?"

"It's me. Mason."

Bank shook his head and rolled his eyes. He hated that his voice was so familiar and gave him at times a weird peace.

"What you want, nigga?"

"I don't want any problems, Banks. I wanna go on the record with that statement. Before we go any further."

"What is that supposed to mean?"

"I don't know what's going to happen with this doctor. But I do know if we put our heads together, we can make sure Ace has the support he needs and convince dude he can—."

"If you're telling me you plan to fight me on custody later then so be it. But I'm not changing my mind. I believe you are the reason he was taken away from me and the moment he's back I won't let you see him again."

"You do realize you sound like a female right? Holding a nigga back from his kids cause you mad."

Banks laughed and shook his head. "I know you meant that to be a slight. And I'm okay with it. But Jersey told me what really happened when the Twins were conceived. So, I'm good."

"And what exactly did she tell you?"

"That her and I were planning to have children using a donor. You got upset and illegally transposed your sperm for the donors with the help of my grandmother. Which was against the law. All I have to do is go through the courts and with that act alone, I'll be granted full rights. When I tell you, I want nothing else to do with you, I need you to understand it's not a game. This is not the Banks you remember."

"And what about you? You're a female, who lived as male, and then became female again, only to become male once more. I mean are you doing wigs or not?"

"Nigga!"

"Oh, let's not forget about your memory loss. How we know you not crazy? Having your two kids in the attic and not even knowing they were there for years. You don't think the courts would find that weird? I was calling you to try to make amends. But I see that's not what you want. So, if it's war, let it be war."

When Banks ended the call, Jersey slid in the bed behind him. Resting the side of her face on his arm she sighed deeply. "Taking a quick nap?"

" I want you to set up a meeting with my oldest children."

"A meeting or dinner? Because if you ask me, you're sounding more like Banks each day." She giggled. "So, I have to be sure."

Banks chuckled once, not entirely certain what she meant by her comment. "Make it dinner. And see if Tinsley is up for it too. He's been sad lately and I want to find out why."

"You got it."

CHAPTER FOUR

PETIT ESTATE

Tinsley walked around the room he held in the Petit mansion. Jersey had asked him about dinner and for the moment he said yes.

Ever since he met Banks, he was able to build a life for himself under his wing, and things looked good.

Financially anyway.

Still, nothing meant more than having a relationship with River, something which he suffered through over the passing months.

Why did she seem to hate him so?

Why couldn't she forgive and slowly forget?

Grabbing his red velvet robe, which felt like a warm massage, he slipped it on and removed his phone off the dresser. Scrolling the screen, he was aggravated when he realized she had not returned any of his calls since he popped over her house.

What made him angry, was not only Flower calling him out as if he had an attraction to River, but also the fact that she ruined her friend's life and he had to help put it back together.

Scrolling through his contacts he dialed a number. "Ahn, ahn, bitch, I know you not calling me after all this time."

Tinsley laughed. "Calm down, Emo."

"Don't tell me to calm down. We ain't heard from you for a month of Sundays. I mean where you been bitch?"

"You know Benji was murdered so it's been a long road."

"Oh my, God, Tin! I didn't know. I'm sorry, girl."

"It's okay."

"How you holding up?"

He flopped on the edge of his bed. "I'm fine. It was an abusive relationship anyway so I'm glad I got away from him. He—."

Emo laughed.

"Fuck is so funny?"

"Wait, you serious?"

Tinsley frowned. "I asked you a question. What is funny?"

"Tinsley, everybody knows you like violent sex. You and Benji stayed going hard in the bedroom. Shit, I remember one night you told us he choked you out so much, you almost died. You also said it was the best dick you ever had in your life. No cap."

"This ain't like that!"

"Okay, girl, okay," Emo laughed. "No need to get mad. Emo ain't mean nothing by it. But I miss your ass anyway."

Tinsley flopped back and looked up at the ceiling. "That's not why I called you though."

"Emo, listening."

He hated when he talked in third person like a children's character. "I need you to run a check on this bitch."

"Sure, she fucking somebody you like?"

"Nah, it ain't like that."

"Oh, because the last person you had me run a check on was fucking Benji and it came back that he was cheating. Ya'll broke up for—."

"See this why I don't like to call you half the fucking time." He sat up. "It's always a fucking game. Can you pull the bitch's deets or not?"

"Okay, girl, you ain't gotta be—."

"That's why I never like hitting you up. It's always some—."

"What's the information then, whore! I don't know what you been up to, but this sensitive shit is a mess."

"It ain't—."

"Just give me the slut's name. And just so you know, the next one is gonna cost you, with your touchy ho ass."

PETIT ESTATE

Walid just finished eating dinner when the Butler walked up to the dining room table and sat down across from him. The light from the chandelier tickled the diamonds around the young king's neck.

"What's wrong this time?"

He sighed. "I'm unhappy."

He nodded. "I need more, Walid."

"My brother." He moved uneasily in his seat. "The lady who tricked him. I'm scared."

"I won't let anything happen to you."

"I'm worried about my brother. Not me."

"You'll both be fine."

He nodded, having trusted the Butler with his whole heart.

"But I need you to be easy with your mother."

"I don't like how she looks. Her hair is too short and—"

"You can't treat your mother mean, Walid. You have to be careful with adults. Respect those who take care of you, until you can take care of yourself. You aren't powerful enough yet. You will be soon though. And when the world meets you, they will bow to you. I see it in your eyes. Do you understand what I mean?"

He nodded. "I think so."

"Everything will work how it supposed to work out. I promise."

CHAPTER FIVE

MINNESOTA'S ESTATE

Minnesota was walking to the table with several champagne flutes when she looked down at her diamond ring. When it caught the light of the chandelier above and sparkled, she realized how beautiful it was. In all of the excitement of learning she was pregnant and getting engaged in the same day, she hadn't savored the moment.

And yet, she finally took in the magnificence of her diamond.

Zercy really went all out.

Walking up behind her, he kissed her on the ear and rubbed her flat belly. "You smell so fucking good." He inhaled and snaked his hands between her legs. Her warmth caressed his fingertips. "I can't wait to taste you tonight."

She giggled. "You always say that."

"And I always eat that shit too." He kissed her on the cheek and looked at the dinner table which was laid out with fancy dinner and silverware. "Everything looks amazing."

"You think they will like it?"

"They'll love it."

"Thank you," she blushed. "It's my first time hosting a dinner party, so I wanted to make sure everything was—."

DING DONG.

"I'll get it," he said as he walked past her and toward the door.

Suddenly Minnesota's heart rate increased. She wanted this moment to be a step in the right direction. In her mind she hoped it would signal unity between her family and the Lou's and she needed it to work.

For everyone involved.

Maybe Mason and Banks could get along too in the future.

Who knows?

"Hey, Minnie!" Shay said walking in with Derrick. "Everything looks amazing! I was thinking we were having hot dogs and shit but now…girl…this is fancy."

Minnesota hugged her and accepted a bottle of wine she was holding, before handing it to Zercy. "Thank you for coming."

"What's this about?" Derrick said, kissing her on the cheek.

"I'll tell you when everyone gets here," she led them to their seats at the table. "Everybody should be coming in any—."

DING DONG.

"I'll get it," Zercy said exiting again.

"Wow, everybody's on time," Minnesota said glancing down at her diamond watch. "This is a first."

"I guess we all wanna know what's going on," Derrick admitted. "Otherwise, we would be late as usual."

"He not lying," Shay said, taking a piece of bread from the table. "With the things that been happening in this family, we still on edge and hoping it's all good news."

When River and Flower walked inside, everyone waved. To be honest Minnesota didn't care for Flower, but Zercy had bonded to River so hard, that they had to respect her girlfriend too.

River bopped over and gave Minnesota a hug, while Flower waved, doing her very best to cling to River like saran wrap per usual.

Ever since Christmas Eve, with the pain they endured upon watching Ace lose reason, River had become a fixture with the family.

And they loved the addition and energy she brought.

Walking over to the table, River shook Derrick's hand, kissed Shay on the cheek and took her seat.

"So, what's up?" River scooted up to the table. Looking around she asked, "Everybody good?"

"We'll tell you in a minute," Zercy said smiling so brightly, he almost gave the secret away.

Five minutes later, his triplet sisters walked inside, and the mood darkened. They threw smiles at all those present, but it was obvious they didn't fuck with anybody but their brother.

Waving at everyone, they sat in their seats. And since they were sitting shoulder to shoulder, they looked like they were conjoined due to their identical faces.

Ten minutes later Joey entered with his wife.

Minnesota and Shay were so happy to see him they almost knocked him over as they rushed him with hugs and kisses.

The reason was real.

Shit was thick with the siblings for a minute.

When Joey learned that they all participated in Banks' conversion to Blaire, he was angry and just like Banks, cut everybody off for a period. After some time, and missing his siblings, he came around. Besides, they had already lost Harris Wales years earlier, and there was no need in staying apart for much longer.

After Minnesota and Shay disconnected from them, they focused on the blond-haired beauty with piercing blue eyes that was at his side. At first, they assumed she was a friend, until they looked down and saw the ring on her finger.

"Oh, I almost forgot," Joey said. "This my wife." He smiled proudly.

Shay frowned. "So ain't no black women wherever you were held up at that rehab place?"

His wife turned beet red.

"Shay, come over here and sit the fuck down!" Derrick yelled from the table. "You always starting shit when we get around people. Embarrassing the fuck outta me like you a lunatic. Sit down!"

"Nigga, shut up!"

Joey shook his head and addressed Shay directly. "First off, you know I ain't got no problem with black women. But this woman is the reason I'm alive today. This woman is the woman who helped me stay off heroin. This woman is the woman who told me I was worth more than drugs. And if you gonna disrespect my wife, by going at her race, despite our father being half white too, then I'ma bounce." He looked at all of them. "So, what ya'll wanna do?"

Minnesota nudged him. "Ain't nobody tripping off your white wife!" She laughed. "Shay was just fucking with you."

Shay could no longer hold her smile and giggled hard. "Boy, relax! I'm just playing. That's what you get for not being around us for so long. Don't know when folks joking."

"If she can put up with our shit, we'll gladly have her." Minnesota chuckled harder and embraced his wife. "Although I can tell you had that speech ready for us too," she continued.

Joey chuckled. "I did. Can't even front."

The room erupted into laughter.

"So, what's your name, wife?" Minnesota asked.

"Sidney," she said in a low voice.

"Sidney Wales." Minnesota nodded. "I like that."

After a few more words, they were shown their seats with the rest. Minnesota on the other hand, stood by the table, with Zercy giving her a side hug. Every so often she would look at her watch and this put Zercy on pause because she seemed sad.

"You okay, sweetheart?" He asked.

She looked at her watch once more. "Yeah, I guess so."

Zercy kissed her lovingly on the forehead and exhaled, while looking at everyone. He was ready to break the news as if it were his idea. "We asked you all here because—."

DING DONG.

Minnesota smiled. "He came," she said excitedly under her breath. "He came!"

"Let me go see who that is."

Zercy rushed to the door and returned with a solemn Spacey. The first person Spacey looked at when he entered the room was Minnesota who smiled. She was so glad he showed up.

Next, Spacey waved at everyone else.

"You okay?" Spacey asked, examining her for injuries.

She nodded. "I'm fine." She grinned. "Thanks for coming, but please sit down."

He handed Zercy a bottle of Hennessey and sat next to Shay who gave him a side hug.

Zercy and Minnesota stood on the side of the table again. "We brought you all here to say, we are getting married," he said.

Cheers and congratulations mixed with excitement filled the room.

From everyone, but Spacey and the triplets.

"We're not done," Minnesota teased raising her hands to quiet everyone down. "I'm also pregnant."

More excitement from everyone but the triplets and Spacey.

"I came out here for this?" Spacey said.

"What, nigga?" Joey said.

"Are you sure about this shit?" Spacey asked Minnesota in a serious tone. "I mean, are you really sure this what you want to do? Because you don't even know this nigga for real for real."

"I agree," Ziamond, one of the triplets said.

"I mean, weren't you pregnant when we met you?" Ziggy, another triplet responded.

"Facts." Zuri, the last triplet cosigned.

"What difference does it make if she was pregnant before?" Shay stated with much attitude and thunder. "We talking about now. If y'all not gonna keep up ya'll can just leave. It's nothing."

"Exactly," Joey responded. "Fuck we care about her getting pregnant back then? She pregnant now." He didn't know she was pregnant in the past, but he wasn't surprised.

He remembered her being loose booty.

"Easy everybody," Zercy said extending palms around. "Tonight, is supposed to be about my fiancé and our future baby. Now we asked you here to take part in that, if you have a problem with it—."

Spacey got up abruptly, stomped across the room and kissed Minnesota on the cheek. "I got a problem with it, but I expect you know that already."

"Why, nigga?" Joey yelled from the table. "Shouldn't you be happy your little sister getting married? I mean, am I missing something?"

It was at that point that the room realized that he wasn't aware that Minnesota and Spacey had sex in the attic of the Petit mansion.

And it was also at that moment that most feared the truth would be revealed and he would erupt violently.

"Just...just let it go, Joey," Minnesota said under her breath, trying her best not to ruin the moment.

"Well, I want this family to get along," Zercy said, seeing the sadness in Minnesota's eyes. "And my fiancé was hoping this could bring us all together."

"The thing is, this family will never come together," River said in all seriousness. "I'm sorry, bruh."

Everyone focused on her.

"Why you say that?" Joey asked.

"Because Mason and Banks are on the verge of war. And everybody in here should be concerned because soon, we all will have to pick a side."

CHAPTER SIX

PETIT ESTATE

Mason paced around his office rapidly, while listening to a recording that he received on the phone. It was from a caller who had an ominous message.

"You will die soon."

That was it.

That was all.

Mason tried to be calm, but whoever was threatening him successfully ruffled his feathers and he didn't have the benefit of any liquor to help.

Picking up his cell, he flopped in his chair and made a call. "You home?"

"Yeah, of, of course I am," Dasher said excitedly. "You coming over? Because I haven't seen you in weeks."

"What you talking about?" He frowned. "I picked up Bolt the other day."

"I'm talking about me. *I* haven't seen you. Are you coming over?"

"Yeah, but I'm trying to hit that pussy too. You with that?"

"I'm with anything you want, Mason. And that's on everything."

"Be naked. Be ready."

He ended the call, grabbed his keys and hit it to his garage to get his truck. Although he wasn't feeling Dasher a hundred percent, what he did like was that she was always available.

But there was another reason for leaving the house, outside of receiving the news that someone was trying to kill him, he was also doing his level best to avoid Morgan.

After returning from her holiday vacation, she had questions about what was going on with the twins, having been given very little information. But Mason simply didn't feel like talking. Besides, although it had been a long time since he had a mother figure in his life, and despite needing one greatly, he wasn't in the mood to hear what was *right*.

He needed someone to be on his side.

He was almost at Dasher's house when he reached a light. Glancing over to the left, he paused when he saw two men sitting in a navy-blue van. But there was a third person in the back, and he couldn't see their face due to the window being tinted so darkly.

"Fuck you looking at?" Mason yelled, on his old hood Baltimore shit.

He thought it was odd that they were staring at him, until one of the men aimed a barrel in his direction.

This was an assassination attempt, he was certain.

"What the fuck!" He ducked.

Although the light was still red, Mason hit the gas and entered the intersection without looking at the road.

He missed two cars and a truck barely as he pushed the Benz truck to its limits. If he was going to die, he had in his mind it wouldn't be on their terms.

He was five miles away, when he felt calm enough to pull over. Grabbing his phone, he called his most trusted.

"River, where you at?" He said huffing and puffing as he stood on the side of the road. "Somebody just tried to kill me."

"Tell me where you are and I'm on my way!"

Twenty minutes later River was standing in front of him. "Mason, this was Banks." She was pacing and her nerves were on edge. "I feel it in my soul." She put her hand over her heart.

"You can't say that." He crossed his arms over his chest and leaned on his truck.

"Who else would want you dead but Banks? You doing good by everybody on the streets and they eating. So, it has to be Banks. Nobody else wanna see you gone.

And niggas know you don't carry paper around no more so it's not robbery."

Mason rushed up to her. "Kid, I love you, you know that. But if you ever mention his name in that way again, we done."

PETIT ESTATE

Banks entered the house where Jersey was standing in the middle of the floor waiting. Yawning, he tossed his keys on the table by the door. "What's wrong? And where is Blakeslee?"

"She's asleep. She wanted to wait up for you, but I told her you may be late getting back. Why you leave out the house like that?"

"I'm tired right now. You gonna give me some pussy or nah?" Banks flopped on the sofa and the Butler walked up to him.

The mood ruined.

"Can I get you anything, sir?"

His booming voice and piercing green eyes scared the fuck out of Jersey every time she saw him.

"We're good," Banks said.

When he left, she sat on Banks' lap, straddling him per usual. "He scares the hell out of me. Why do you keep the same staff? I mean, aren't they the same people who were here when Minnie and Spacey were in the attic?"

"He's definitely not for everybody. But since he makes Walid happy, I keep him around." He dragged a hand down his face. "Plus he was only doing what Gina demanded. I got rid of the maid though. I never trusted her ass."

"I hope your judgement is not blind with him and you're just holding onto Gina by keeping him here." She sighed. "Anyway, the hypnotist called again. She's wondering when you will restart the sessions since you made so much progress. I told her—."

"I don't think I'm going to continue."

"What? Why?" She threw her hands up in the air. "I can tell since you've been using her that you're more like yourself. Maybe you should—"

"Memories, Jersey. I need my memories, all of them and she's not able to do it in the way I want. So why waste more time and money?"

"Banks, you rich as fuck! So I think that's a major mistake. She said that something may occur which will give you all your old memories. Maybe we have to wait on that before—."

"I made my mind up," he said firmly, giving her looks that could kill. "Leave it alone."

She sighed. "I want to ask you something, and I want you to be honest."

"You know I hate when you do that."

"Banks, please…"

"What is it?"

"When will you stop hating me?"

He frowned. "I don't—."

"I know you don't trust me, and I wanna know why? Let's keep it real."

"You want real?"

"I deserve it!"

"Because you went along with the big lie," he shrugged. "You knew who I was, and you stole time from me by lying. Time, I needed to restart my life. For years in this house, I knew something was off, and to think that you knew too, and you didn't tell me the truth, it really enrages me."

She looked down. "I knew you still hated me for my part in it all. And you're right."

"If you know I'm right, why ask the fucking question?"

"I guess, I don't know, I guess I want to know if we'll ever have a future. If you don't want me, tell me." She placed a warm hand on his face. "But tell me now. Because lately, I been thinking of my life. I been thinking of Howard. And if me and you don't make a go of it, maybe I'll just try and find him. Maybe I'll go away."

He looked out. "I want you here. But that's gonna have to be good enough for now, Jersey."

She nodded and sighed for what seemed like forever. The men she had in her life always drained her soul. Leaving her with whatever was left.

"By the way, I talked to all your kids. About the dinner you want to host."

"Well?"

"They were actually all together tonight. Minnesota's getting married and so she wanted to let them know."

"Really?" He smiled, for the first time in a long time.

"Yep, and she's pregnant too."

Banks nodded. "That's good. I want her happy." He sighed. "I want all of them happy. I just...you know..."

"I know." She nodded. "You wish what happened didn't happen with Mason. And I'm sure I speak for all of them when I say we are all on your time. We will get through this, Banks. As a family. I'm not going anywhere. Take all the time you need."

He nodded. "Thank you."

She kissed his cheek. "So, where were you tonight again?"

Banks' phone rang, and this time he saw who was on the other side. "What you want, Mason?"

"We gotta talk! So I'ma need you to stop dodging me, my nigga! Now!"

CHAPTER SEVEN

PREACH'S ABANDONED HOUSE

Preach and Michigan were standing up in the basement of one of Preach's rehab houses looking down at Natty. At first, she was hopeful that the evening would end with all things going well. She figured the most he would have for her were a few questions and accusations. But upon looking at the stress on his face, she could no longer say the same.

He was giving off madman tendencies.

"I don't know what you want from me?" She yelled up at him. "I've told you all I fucking know!"

"I want to know what's going on with you and Hercules. And I want to know if Carmen has been around."

"I don't know what he's doing, but I promise you that I haven't spoken to her. I don't know anything about her. Why don't you ask him instead of bothering me? You have to—."

"I don't have to do shit, bitch!" He yelled. "Do you hear me? Nothing!"

Both Natty and Michigan realized at that moment he was off the hinges. It was obvious that she had to handle him with ease.

"Preach, you are a better man than this. I know you are. Back in the day, you were always so smart. Can't you tell when I'm telling the truth?"

"I don't wanna hear no—."

"I'm pregnant!"

"You think I care about some white boy squeezing off up in you?"

"No, but you should know that the baby in my womb is Banks' direct bloodline. And if you hurt me, you hurt our child. Is that what you think Banks wants?"

"You smell like Hennessy." He glared.

Now she wished she hadn't bothered with the drink. "I don't drink."

"Actually, I smell it on you too," Michigan shrugged. "Just didn't wanna say nothing after you said you were pregnant and all."

"And like I said, I wouldn't give a fuck if you were carrying his baby or not, what I do know is this, you will tell me what you know about Carmen. Or shit will get bad for you, Natty. Because at this point, I have nothing to lose. NOTHING!" He looked at his goon. "Gag this bitch until she's ready to talk. Because she ain't saying shit yet."

EMO'S APARTMENT

Emo was frying chicken for his man, which was his neighbor's husband with one hand, and scrolling the internet on his laptop with the other. When he finally saw what he was looking for, he almost burned the chicken.

For his efforts, smoke spilled out everywhere in the apartment.

"I know that better not be my food in there!" Bill yelled from the living room after smelling burn scents. "Because I'm sick of bad meals around this bitch!"

Emo was about to answer using his own deep voice, until he realized he preferred high pitches and feminine tones. Clearing his throat, he said, "It's fine, baby. Emo will give you the lighter pieces."

"Mannnn." He said irritated. "This some bullshit." At one point Emo was one of the best cooks in the world, which is how he lured him from across the hall.

But now he was undercover trash.

Unconcerned, Emo waved the air and made notes with what he was seeing on his laptop. After he pulled up all the information he could, he made a call. "Hey, girl, what you doing?"

"Getting ready for bed, why?" Tinsley said yawning on the other line.

"I found the information you needed." Emo grabbed the chicken out of the pan and dropped it onto the napkin layered plate.

Grease droplets splattered everywhere.

Just nasty.

"Well, is it good or bad?"

"Put your shit on. I'll be there in twenty minutes so you can see for yourself."

Thirty minutes later, Tinsley and Emo were watching Flower standing outside of a worn-out brick apartment building. She was talking to a man and in Tinsley's opinion, they were too close for comfort.

"Is that her husband?" Emo asked, from the passenger side of his red two-seated Mazda Miata.

"I don't know who that nigga is." Tinsley said as he glared out the tinted window. "All I know is that I knew I couldn't trust that bitch. And now I'm finding out I was right."

"I don't know about you, but I would tell River A.S.A.P. Because on paper, it says she's married. I verified that shit. And if she's married that damn sure means she ain't single."

Tinsley nodded and sighed.

Emo looked over at him. "Fuck is you so quiet for? I thought you wanted the deets on that whore. Shouldn't you be celebrating? Hell, that's why Emo wanted to bring you over here. So, I could watch you gloat."

"I'm happy."

"So why doesn't it seem like it?" He threw his red manicured nails up in the air. "You dry as shit in here."

"Because I don't want to hurt River's feelings either. I mean look at that bitch. This is the one person she can't seem to get out of her heart." He focused on Flower again. "How will it be if I tell her that the love of her life is still a fake?"

"Tinsley, you can't—."

"I'm serious. I don't want to break her. I just want her to leave that slut alone."

Emo leaned back and looked at him closer. "Why do I have a feeling you into fish? Like, fish, fish."

His eyebrows rose. "What the fuck are you talking about?"

"I wasn't sure at first, but now I know that whoever this chick River is, you are into her. What is she? A Dom? An AG? What is it? Because whatever it is, it better be masculine so I can at least understand. You over here —."

"This is about me wanting to protect my friend. Nothing more and nothing less. So, keep your conclusions to yourself."

"Maybe it's something else," Emo said pointing at him. "But something feels off to me."

"Like what?"

"Maybe you don't like River in that way, or whatever her name is." Emo focused on Flower a bit more. "Maybe you're just afraid of the damage this girl can cause. Whatever it is, I can see the fear all in your eyes. And I'm scared for you too."

CHAPTER EIGHT

RIVER'S APARTMENT

River and Flower were getting ready for bed when Flower laid her head gently on River's chest. "What's on your mind, pretty girl?" River asked.

Flower inhaled and exhaled, her breath smelling like mint due to brushing her teeth. "I don't know, it's like, I mean, can I give you my opinion on something?"

River turned the lamp on and looked down at her. "What is it?"

Flower sat up in bed, her knees pulled closely against her chest. And since she wasn't wearing panties, the window to her pussy was wide open.

"I don't want to overstep my boundaries, but something you said resonated with me when we were at Minnesota's house."

"What is it?"

"When we were at dinner and you said that Banks and Mason would never be friends. I think you're right. I think you even mentioned war."

River sat up with her back against the baseboard. "Okay, what made you bring that up?"

She sighed. "I don't want to talk about it because I know it's not my place but at the same time—."

"Flower, what's on your fucking mind? Stop playing games with me. It's been a long day and all I wanna do is rest."

She sighed, already feeling like she was getting on her nerves. "Do you remember when you saw me and Shay talking in the foyer? At Mason's house."

"Yeah, so what?"

"Well, we were talking about a conversation she overheard with Banks and Joey. And I'm not certain, but I think Banks is plotting something on Mason's head. Something about hitting him when he least expects it.

That's why I was surprised Shay stayed quiet when you mentioned war."

She frowned and jumped out of bed. "What...what you saying?"

"I'm telling you what she overheard."

"Well why she feel comfortable telling you? She just met you! And why are you just telling me now? You not supposed to keep nothing from me no more, bitch. Ever! Is you out of your mind?"

Flower jumped due to her anger.

"Because I...I...I didn't think everybody would be linking up with each other again. The Lou's and the Wales. I mean, you said they would probably stop being so close after Christmas and —."

River started getting dressed.

"What are you doing?" Flower yelled with wide eyes.

"I'm about to warn Mason."

Flower's stomach swirled as she scooted off the bed. It was so quick she gave her butt cheeks rug burn. "Wait, what are you going to tell him?"

"What you mean? I'm going to tell him what you just told me."

Flower wanted to faint.

Throw the dirt on her face already.

"River, what the fuck are you talking about?" She paced quickly. "If you tell him that what do you think will happen to me?"

"What you saying? Because I'm not going to let him get hurt!"

"I get it but think about it. If it comes back that I told you a conversation that I had with Shay, one that I promised I would keep in confidence, they will never like or trust me. They may even kill me. And it would be all your fault." She pointed a short finger her way.

River paused, while holding her shoes in her hand. She heard Flower, no doubt, but when it came to Mason she simply did not play. So, she had to move smartly with the information she just learned.

Slowing down, she dropped the shoes and grabbed her hand. Pulling her next to her on the edge of the bed she said, "Are you sure about what Shay told you?"

Flower frowned, "Wait, why would you ask me something like that?"

River glared and moved closer. "I'm gonna ask you again, are you sure that Shay said Banks is putting a hit on Mason's head? And let me be clear, if I find out you wrong, breaking up will be the least of your worries."

Up until that point Flower assumed River was green for her. And for the most part, her heart did beat with her name. But in that moment, it was obvious that Mason had taken first place and that made Flower hate Mason even more.

"I'm not lying."

"I never said you were lying, but I am asking if you're sure. Because shit like this can cause problems that you can't even imagine."

Flower could tell at that moment that River had grown up. And so, she needed to dig into her old bag of tricks. She needed to do something that always worked no matter what in the past.

So, she toppled on the floor and started crying.

Arms flailing, pussy wide open as her legs tossed around in the air.

River, caught off guard, lowered her height and helped her back to the bed. Sitting at her side again she rubbed her back. "Calm down, yo. Fuck is you doing?"

"I can't believe I said anything to you," Flower sniffled. "You're turning on me! You're fucking turning on me!"

River took a deep breath. "It's not that, bae. It's just that, you know what, lets drop it. I'll get up with Mason, but I won't tell him you said anything. Okay?"

"You promise?"

"If I'm saying it, then it's my word."

She sniffled a few more times and sighed. "I just don't want anything happening to you, River. That's the only reason I told you, I swear."

"I know." River smiled and rubbed her back. "You want something to drink?"

Flower nodded. "A coke with ice."

River rose and walked toward the door, but when Flower looked in the direction she exited, she caught her glaring her way before she walked off.

The look gave Flower chills.

CHAPTER NINE

CHILDREN'S HOSPITAL

The psychiatrist was determined and decided that nothing would stop him from getting some of the answers to his questions that afternoon. And he could tell by how tense Mason, Banks and Jersey appeared that it would be a long day.

"Before we start, I need to know how is my son," Banks said plainly. "Because doc, I'm getting very agitated."

"And we know how you are when you get agitated," Mason laughed once, throwing darts.

Banks chuckled. "So, because I resist your request for drinks, you still mad, nigga? Get over it, dummy."

"Everybody please, relax." The doctor cleared his throat. "He's calmer."

"Calmer?" Mason repeated. "We specifically said we don't want him on drugs. I know you aren't disrespecting our wishes. We—."

"This isn't about drugs."

"Okay, so what is it about?"

"It's about him getting back into the routine. He doesn't lash out as much. Even plays with toys and at the same time, he appears confused on why he's here."

Jersey wiped her hair out of her face. "Then I'm confused on why he's here too. What are you saying?"

"I think he forgot what he did. On Christmas Eve."

Mason smirked. "So, you're saying he can't remember wielding a knife in the living room for—."

"Yes. He doesn't remember. I've seen this kind of thing happen before with young children. Especially in those who are abused by their—."

"I never abused my son!" Mason yelled pointing his way. "Ever!"

"I didn't say that. I was saying that the patterns are the same. They forget to protect their minds."

"All I know is this, if he's forgotten why he's here, then what is he still doing in this facility?" Jersey asked. "Let us bring him home."

The psychiatrist looked at the trio harder.

And suddenly all became clear to Mr. Wales.

"So, you don't trust us," Banks said. "At the end of the day, you're judging us based on what happens here. Based on how we act in this office."

"It's not about trust. It's about the welfare of —."

"There is no place else for my son to be, except home!" Banks yelled. "This is no place for him to grow up! You barely let us see him. How much longer do you think I'll let you keep him here?"

"Is that a threat?"

Banks smiled.

"Listen, I'm only hesitating because last time you saw him, he…he…seemed —."

"He got upset about how Banks looks." Mason said with a grin on his face. Still wondering if Banks was responsible for trying to kill him a few days ago, he was definitely on some get back shit. Even if he tried to tell River he didn't believe it was him.

"Yes." The doctor said. "Banks' appearance definitely made him upset."

Banks looked down. "So, I'm supposed to change for him? I'm supposed to wear a dress and a wig?"

"No, I didn't say that."

"Because he has to stay true to who he is," Jersey interjected, wanting all of the coolness that was Banks to remain the exact same. "And with time, Ace will learn to get used to it."

"You mean like Walid got used to it?" Mason said slyly.

They all looked at him.

"Fuck is that supposed to mean?" Jersey asked.

"I know Walid has a problem with Banks putting on as a man too."

"Putting on as a man?" Banks snapped. "If you hadn't lied about me being female, you would've been taking this dick." He said, gripping the strap in his pants.

"What, nigga?" Mason yelled, wanting to shoot him on sight for the comment.

"Everybody sit down!" The doctor yelled.

"All I'm saying if it's no big deal, then it shouldn't be a problem with Walid either. Right? So is Walid okay with it or not?"

"You're going to regret trying to come between me and my son." Banks said. "I promise you; you will regret it."

Mason laughed. "Is that right?"

Banks remained silent as he glared his way.

"Let's be clear on what I need right now," the psychiatrist interjected. "I need to understand a little

154   *Truce 3: Sins of The Fathers*

more about your backgrounds. Because something in this family has triggered Ace. And every time I try to go there, a fight breaks out between the three of you. Which makes me believe I'm sure the nucleus of the issue is right in this room. Unfortunately for Ace, I cannot make an assessment to release him to either of you until I find what I need to know."

Banks moved uneasily in his seat.

Mason slumped lower.

And Jersey crossed her legs, as she wiggled her foot anxiously.

"What do you want to know?" Banks asked.

"Tell me about your father."

"I don't remember mine."

He sat back in his chair. "So, you don't remember anything about your past?"

"I told you that on day one." Banks said. "And I'm getting the impression that you don't believe me."

"I would never presume to —."

"Like I said before, I don't remember my past."

"What about your mother?"

"Nothing." Banks looked down. "I remember nothing."

The doctor nodded again and focused on Mason. "What about your parents?"

"My father was a drug dealer. My mother was not in my life. And yet it didn't stop me from being a good father to my children."

Jersey smirked and giggled forward in her seat.

"Fuck is so funny?" He leaned over and asked.

"What did I tell you about speaking to her directly?" Banks asked.

Mason was getting heated. And he couldn't pinpoint what made him angrier. But it was between the way Banks coveted her and the way Jersey talked to him directly. As if she was anything more than an incubator. As if he didn't fuck her up back in the day for the disrespect.

Mason focused on the psychiatrist.

"Regardless of what my ex-wife says, I was a good father. And I didn't allow any of my father's shortcomings to impact how I raised my other kids. Or how I'm raising Ace and Walid and how I will be raising Bolt."

"This ain't about Bolt, nigga," Banks said. "You can keep Bolt."

Mason glared.

The doctor knew he couldn't get anywhere with them and so he changed course. Instead, his suspicions were raised even higher. "That'll be enough for today. But you all can come with me."

After the meeting, he took them to see Ace, per their request.

And the moment Banks saw a subdued Ace, his heart thumped. Mason and Jersey weren't doing much better looking at a fraction of who the boy was before entering the facility.

Bad as hell, but full of life.

So, whose kid was that?

The child was sitting in a chair, with no television on, looking at the wall. His expression was between sadness and indifference.

"Fuck is wrong with my son?" Mason yelled at the doctor's face.

"I told you he's calm now."

"That's not calm!" Banks said pointing at the glass wall. "That's...that's sadness."

"We want to talk to him." Mason said seriously.

"Now!" Banks yelled.

"Okay, before we go in there, I have a few ground rules."

"I want to see my son!" Banks yelled, nostrils flaring. "No more rules!" He stepped closer. "You don't know who I am, so you better be careful with me."

That was scary.

"First, all of this animosity, cannot go on in there. We do not want him to think that the world he might be returning to, will be as volatile as it was before he left." He paused. "Do you all understand?"

They nodded yes.

"Good, and the second thing is, let him come to you. No pressuring him or anything like that. Do you agree?"

They nodded again, just to get the man up out of their faces.

The doctor looked at the glass and waved at the social worker who was in the room with him. The moment they walked inside, Mason first, Ace's eyes lit up. Slowly he got out of his chair and walked toward him.

Banks hated seeing him stripped of his iced-out jewels.

Wrapping his arms around his legs, he looked up to Mason and said, "I wanna come home."

"Soon, son." He said.

Banks stepped inside and in a low voice said, "Hey, Big Man."

Ace stared at him for a minute, and then, as if he'd given up fighting, he hugged him too. "Hi, mommy."

It was awkward for the social worker and the psychiatrist to hear him call such a masculine being mommy, but Banks didn't care. Just as long as he opened the lines of communication with him, Banks would take it.

"Hi, son. How do you feel?"

"Are you here to take me home? Please…I don't like it here anymore."

They all spent what time they had left ensuring Ace that soon it would all be over. And afterwards Banks left angrier than he had been before he arrived. He blamed the world, Mason and more than anything Carmen for the separation.

And he wanted blood.

Once in the passenger seat of his car, with Jersey steering, he called Preach. "Did you find Carmen?" He barked into the phone.

Whether Banks remembered the past or not, it was obvious that he was returning to his old mannerisms.

"Not yet. Maybe Hercules might—."

"I already talked to him! I told you that!" He roared. "You're doing shit that I can do on my own! He says he doesn't know."

"But I've been looking—."

"You got 72 hours. Not an hour more! Do you hear me? Not one fucking hour more!"

CHAPTER TEN

PREACH'S REHAB HOUSE

Preach sat in his car, with the cell phone still in hand. After hearing the hatred in Banks' voice, he knew there was no way he would accept anything other than where Carmen was located.

Which at the time was information he didn't have in his possession.

Parked in front of the rehab house that held Natty, he eased out the car. He couldn't make it two feet before throwing up on the side of his vehicle. To say Banks got in his mind was an understatement.

Still, he determined in that moment that he was going to get answers from Natty, even if he had to kill her first. Even if he made her lie, just to tell Banks something.

He was going to do just that.

She really was the only connection in his mind to Carmen. He would've snatched Hercules too, but something told him uncles were off limits.

Wiping his mouth with the back of his hand, he looked from where he stood and crept behind the house. When he was certain the coast was clear, he opened the back door and descended down the stairs.

The dank basement smell hit him in the nose immediately and for a moment he felt bad for Natty, until he realized that she was sleeping with the enemy.

Walking down the hall leading to where he kept her, he said, "Okay, you gonna have to tell me where she is or..."

His words were paused in his throat when he saw her lying on the floor with her eyes opened, and the gag stuffed in her mouth with dried foam oozing out.

Natty was dead.

She wouldn't be telling him anything ever again.

Rushing up to her, he removed the gag which choked the life out of her body. He tried to resuscitate her, but no matter how many pumps to the chest, in the end she was still gone.

Her skin was cold to the touch.

"No, no, no!" He yelled flopping on the floor. "Please don't be dead! Please don't be dead!"

After what seemed like forever, and after feeling the shooting pain coursing through his wrists, he trudged upstairs more defeated than ever.

Flopping in the passenger seat of his car, he tried to catch his breath. For a second he played back the tapes in his mind of when he held Carmen in his custody. Of when he kidnapped her to get information on the Petit's. It was the very same house that held Natty.

How different life would have been if he had killed Carmen instead of forgetting about her.

How much better life would have been if he hadn't dropped the ball.

But that didn't matter.

He didn't take care of business and so it was over.

Grabbing his cell phone from his pocket, he called his wife. "Hey, beautiful. What you doing?"

"Somebody in a good mood..." she said sexily, loving his playful energy. "I like that shit a lot." Besides, he had been on edge ever since being charged with finding Carmen, and she missed her husband.

"I love you."

"I love you too."

He nodded and took a deep breath. "Remember the house I was telling you about? The one with the red door in the back."

"You mean the one with Carmen and —."

"No, the one in Virginia. The one I saw us living in eventually with the tree that blooms with —."

"Preach what's going on?"

"Listen to me."

"No, I want you to tell me what the fuck is up! Now!"

"She's dead, baby. Natty is dead."

Silence.

"What? H…how?" He heard her gasp. "Baby, no, why did you, why did you do that before—."

"It wasn't me." He dragged a hand down his face. "I went away for a night and when I came back, she was, she was gone. I think she choked on the gag. Michigan must've forced it in her mouth too deep."

"So, what are you gonna do?" She yelled.

"I don't know. I mean—."

"Don't tell Banks."

"Wait, what if he knows I had her and—."

"Listen to me, nothing will come good out of you telling Banks she's dead. And I know you think I don't know what I'm talking about, but I do, baby. And this time you gonna have to trust me."

"But—."

"He thinks Carmen is responsible for everything. And what if he thinks that Natty knew where she could possibly be since Hercules wasn't giving any info? So, telling him she's gone will make things worse."

Preach hated feeling unsure. Normally he was smart enough to handle what happened next. But he wasn't dealing with his old friend. He was dealing with a hybrid that looked like Banks but didn't understand how close they were in the past.

And that put him at a disadvantage.

"Baby, I know you think I don't know any better. But I'm begging you. I'm begging you, not to tell him. Besides, you're the only one who knows you had her there right?"

Silence.

"Right?"

"No..."

"Then if I were you, I would take out everybody who knows. I'm so serious about this shit that even if you think I'll rat, I say kill me too."

CHAPTER ELEVEN

HERCULES' ESTATE

Hercules circled his bedroom floor, as he desperately tried to find out where Natty was located. With his cell phone pressed against his ear, he said, "I don't know where you are, but if you out there acting immature, I'm going to be done with you. Do you hear me? Done!"

When his maid knocked on the door, he sighed and said, "Come in."

A middle-aged white woman entered. "Dinner is ready. Are you —."

"I'm not hungry." He dragged a hand down his face.

Where was his sweet, wet, brown, Natty?

"Well, is there anything I can do for you?"

"No."

She was about to walk out when she doubled back. "Oh, I almost forgot, Mrs. Hide wants you to call her when you get a chance. She sounds pretty upset."

"My dog is still at the vet so she can't say it's barking. She's probably just complaining about shit as usual and —."

"She said it was about your friend."

"What friend?"

"The girl." She walked out.

Confused, he quickly picked up his cell and made a call. Within seconds Cynthia Hide was on the line. "What's going on?"

"What kind of people are you dealing with over there?" The old woman yelled. "Can you at least tell me that?"

Hating her annoying voice, he rolled his eyes and flopped on the side of the bed. "What are you talking about now?"

"I saw your friend get in the car with two men. And I am not comfortable with that sort of element in this neighborhood. We are respectful people, with respectful tendencies."

Hercules rushed to his window to see if he saw Natty's car. When he realized it wasn't there, he sighed. "Wait, what are you talking about again?"

"Like I said, I saw that little girl you run with get into the car with two men. Later on, I saw one of the men come back and get that car she was driving. Now this neighborhood was safe before—."

She talked too loudly.

He hung up and rushed to his video room which held all of his surveillance equipment. After thirty minutes, when he saw Natty being taken away by a man, his heart dropped.

Natty wasn't being immature.

She was kidnapped.

And he saw Preach's face on the screen.

SPACEY'S ESTATE

Spacey was moving the last of his boxes out of the home he once shared with Lila.

They were finally calling it quits and getting a divorce.

After what was a painful day, mainly for his wife, she was having a harder time letting go.

"Those are my towels, Spacey," Lila said, as she stood in the hallway using a walker. Her new man was at her side, rubbing her big back lovingly.

Spacey shrugged and dropped the towels on a chair and grabbed another box marked with Riot's name. The man was rich, he could buy more.

"And my son is not staying over there forever." She continued. "Just so you know."

"Lila, you can barely take care of yourself. Look at you. You're using a walker and your ass ain't been cleaned properly in —."

"That's her son!" Her man interrupted pointing a finger. "You don't get to…"

Spacey's eerie smile put him on pause. He was so shook, that there was something about it that made him walk away, leaving his so-called woman alone.

When he was gone, Spacey walked up to Lila.

"You hate me." She whispered. "You made me this way and you…you hate me." She shook her head slowly. "I mean, don't you Wales' feel any remorse? For anybody other than yourselves? Ever?"

He thought about it for a second and said, "Nah."

"Wow."

Standing directly in front of her, he looked her square in the eyes. "I let you bring a man into my house, because let's be real, you disgust me. I let you have our home, paid in full, because I bought a bigger one. But make no mistake, when it comes to my son, I will bury you both before I let you have him. Are we clear?"

She nodded slowly.

"Oh, and if you see someone hanging around the house strange, hit my phone. I'll make sure someone gets over here ASAP. Wouldn't want you and your little mans back there getting hurt."

He picked up the box and walked out the door, leaving her alone.

CHAPTER TWELVE

LOUISVILLE ESTATE

Mason was sitting in his office with a lot on his mind. Hearing Ace say he wanted to go home, rubbed him the wrong way, and he was determined to see him grow up, even if it meant killing his friend, and at one time the love of his life, Banks Wales.

He was about to make a call once more, before making a move on Banks, when his house manager walked inside his office.

Far from being in the mood, he sighed and shook his head. "Now is not the right time, Morgan. I been—."

"How are you?" She asked in a voice that always put him at ease.

"I'm fine." He grabbed a sheet on his desk, any sheet, to appear busy.

"Listen, I wanted to talk to you about—."

"I really can't rap, Morgan."

"I had a dream about you, Mason. And it's a dream that I have to tell you about, otherwise I won't be able to sleep at night."

He threw the papers down and leaned back in his leather chair. It rocked with his weight. "What was this dream about or whatever?"

"I saw your death."

He sat up slowly and his eyes widened. Originally on his disrespectful shit, now he was all ears. "You saw my death? Is that what you said?"

She nodded.

"Why would you come in here and say something like that to me?"

"I didn't want to. Trust me. And at the same time, I realized I had no choice."

"And what was this death?"

"The details are not necessary."

He shook his head and laughed once, although he found nothing funny. "So, you won't tell me how I'm going to die? Even if it means I can protect myself."

"You were gunned down. I see bullets. And a beautiful sky."

Considering what happened the other night, he was definitely listening now. But as of yet, all he knew was that he would die on a beautiful day.

"So, what can I do? Since you bringing all of this bullshit to my feet, what can I do to save myself?"

"You have to clear your surroundings."

He frowned. "What does that mean?"

"I don't know."

Mason scratched his head. "Well do you have a face? Because I don't know what I'm supposed to do with this info to tell you the truth."

"Mason, my purpose of coming here was not to make you upset. It was to give you information that may help you in the future. That's all I can say. Dinner is ready if you are hungry." With that she walked out, leaving him stuck.

Believing Banks was the purpose of it all, he called his cell again, even though he may send him to voicemail. When he answered he said, "We need to talk. So, either you meet me out, or I'm coming over your crib. Decide!"

SHARK BAR

It was more crowded than what should be the norm per the virus, but still.

Mason was standing in the restaurant, at the bar waiting on Banks. Considering the fact that he already believed someone was trying to kill him before talking to Morgan, after talking to her his nerves were worse than ever.

When his cell rang, he answered. "Where you at? Because you late."

"This River. Who you waiting on?"

He shook his head. "Look, kid, I can't talk right now."

"Well let me be quick. I don't trust Banks."

He frowned. "I thought I told you not to bring up his name again in that way. Didn't we just have this conversation?"

She would not be moved. "I don't trust him. Where are you, Mason?"

"I'm at the Shark Bar. And why don't you trust him this time? Because you told me this already."

"Because I think he has bad intentions. And I know you don't believe me, or even want to hear it but I heard he..."

She continued to talk but he couldn't decipher her words because Banks walked inside, and as a result, all of the attention was on his old friend instead. Even a few females stopped what they were doing to gawk at him.

Mason was also relieved to see he was alone and without his right-hand whore Jersey. "Listen, Kid, hold that thought. I have to go."

"Mason, you —."

He hung up and met Banks halfway.

CHAPTER THIRTEEN

MINNESOTA'S ESTATE

Spacey, Joey and Minnesota were in Minnie's living room, talking about the plan for dinner with Banks the next day. It was obvious that all were on edge about getting together with their Pops after so long.

Even Joey.

"...and I'm not saying to be fake," Joey said to them as he sipped his whiskey. "But just pretend like you understand why he was mad at both of you. Can you both at least do that?"

"What is the purpose of this again?" Spacey shrugged.

"Because if he's reaching out, it's obvious he wants to make things right." Joey continued. "And we don't want him to feel awkward."

"I'm not being fake," Minnesota said, as she sipped her tea. "But if I have something on my mind, I'm going to say it."

"Me too." Spacey said.

"And the point of that is what?" Joey asked. "I'm just saying."

"It's about finally being me." Minnesota said. "Finally being true. Look, last time I let Mason steal my words and thoughts away for his purposes. Pops got mad. And I can't lie, but I wanted Pops to be Blaire. I wanted a mother. And I paid for that by him hating me."

"But you had a mother already," Joey said. "Why did you want another one?"

"Let her talk!" Spacey yelled.

"Why you taking up for her all of a sudden? Minnesota used to be annoying to you. What changed?"

Spacey and Minnesota looked at one another.

A lot changed.

"I'm just saying, if you want things to go smoothly, we have to be ourselves." Spacey said. "And that means being real like she said."

Minnesota took a deep breath. "Like I was saying, if we're going to have dinner, which I want, I will be myself. Whatever that means. And I hope you understand, Joey."

"This is going to go bad," Joey said rubbing his hand down his face. "I have a feeling it's going to be bad."

"Bad how?" Spacey said.

"For starters ya'll niggas looking for get back. And I want my family back. I want the Wales' back."

"Ain't nobody say we looking for get back."

"Spacey, you don't have to tell me. It's obvious. For the past few years, it's been about everybody else but Pops. And now I want it to be about him for five seconds and it's a problem?"

When the triplets appeared in the entryway of the living room, everyone looked at them. "Where is my brother?" Ziamond asked.

"He's out back." Minnesota said nodding toward the rear of the house.

"Doing what?"

"How 'bout you go see for yourself," Joey said with an attitude. He didn't like naire one of them bitches. "Don't you see us talking?"

Ziamond smirked at him. "You know what, it's nice to see the three of you all together."

"Meaning?" Joey said.

"Well, considering your brother fucked your sister and got her pregnant." Ziggy said. "I mean, you're taking it good, because if it was me, I couldn't do it."

Joey's drink dropped from his hand and Minnesota wondered why would Zercy tell them such a sensitive secret. She had a feeling they knew at dinner, based on the comment, but now it was confirmed.

"Fuck are you talking about?" Joey asked standing up.

The triplets smirked and Ziamond said. "Nah, we said enough. Ya'll enjoy the rest of your little day though." She winked and they walked away.

Joey stomped up to both of them. "Somebody tell me what the fuck is she talking about?"

"Man, don't listen to — ."

"Tell me something now," he said cutting Spacey off.

THE SHARK BAR

Banks and Mason were sitting at the bar. Mason nursing a coke and Banks a glass of whiskey.

"…I have to do what I have to do, but it's difficult." Mason said shaking his head. "I just think it's time."

"Shouldn't be hard," Banks shrugged. "If you love her, give her what she wants. Make it official."

"It's not that easy."

"You said you don't wanna be in the streets no more." Banks shrugged. "You said you want to live a life of calm and—."

"I do."

"So, marry, Dasher if you want her so much. It's as simple as that." Banks swallowed every last drop in his glass and beckoned another. He drank all of that too. "Now, what do you want from me, Mason? This meeting is about something and Dasher ain't it."

He nodded. "It's about the Twins."

"What about them?"

"I think we should be the best parents we can be, so that they grow up happy, healthy and sane. And that means me being involved in their lives."

Banks glared. "You won't be around the Twins when this is all said and done."

"Where do you think you can go on this earth that I wouldn't find you?"

"I have more money than you. And that means more ways."

"Banks, I was wrong at how I treated you back then. And I know you don't wanna…"

Banks looked away and Mason noticed. "How come you can't look at me, unless you're mad or I'm not looking at you?"

Banks shook his head and smiled. "Yeah, whatever, nigga."

"Nah, I wanna know."

"Mason, I ain't gotta look at you to make you feel me."

"So, if that's true look at me. Right now."

Banks slowly turned his head, looked at him and then looked down. "I don't know the purpose of this."

"The purpose of this, is that you still give a fuck. And if you still give a fuck, I'm asking that you don't take a permanent action, for a temporary situation. We will get through this, if we stop beefing. Because at the end of the day, you don't want anything to happen to me."

Now he looked at him. "You don't know what I want."

Chills.

"Are you trying to kill me, Banks?"

Silence.

"Banks, are you trying to kill me?"

"Why would you ask me something like that?"

"Answer the question. Honestly."

Banks chuckled once. "Living foul out there huh?"

"Are you trying to kill me or not?"

"I'm not going to answer that question. Period."

"It's a simple yes or no answer."

Banks raised his glass and sipped lightly after having it refilled again. "And it's a question I won't dignify with a response. The only thing we have to talk about is this…are you willing to give over custody to boys you had no right to in the first place? Or does shit have to get nasty?"

"You still talking about dumb shit? Didn't I just say I will be in their lives?"

"How is it dumb? Me and the woman I loved was —."

"You and my wife went behind my back, planned to have children and then got mad when I got in the mix. I'm the victim in that scenario not you!"

"Right, because once again it wasn't about you. And since it wasn't about you, you react like you always do." He took another sip. "Aggressive."

"How do you know how I acted if you can't remember?"

Banks glared. "The only thing I want to make clear is this, nothing will separate me from my boys. And if you try to, I will stop you so help me God."

CRAB SHACK

River was across the street, at another bar, with her eyesight on Mason and Banks from afar. Shit looked heated, before calming down a bit. Although he didn't authorize her to be eavesdropping, after speaking to Flower there was no way she would allow anybody to take Mason from her watch.

She was still surveilling them while drinking a Corona when her phone rang. "River, its me."

She shook her head. "I'm busy."

"Please don't hang up!" Tinsley begged. "We need to talk."

River started to send him on his way, but in her heart of hearts, she missed him and wanted the distraction as she watched Mason.

And so, instead of talking to him on the phone, she gave him the address to where she was posted up.

Twenty minutes later, Tinsley showed up in drag, looking so much like a woman, it sucked River's breath away. And because he was drop dead gorgeous, he caught stares from around the bar, none thinking he was anything other than female.

"I'm so glad you invited me to come, River." He said rubbing the top of his glass with his fingertip. "I hate to keep sounding like a broken record, but still. It feels good talking to you. I miss you so fucking much, River. Please, can we at least try to get back to the old days?"

"Leave it alone." River said as she kept looking at him and then Mason across the street. "It's nothing."

"Seriously. I mean, don't you miss all the fun we used to have?" Tinsley said. "Remember when we used to be in the apartment and — ."

"Maybe I'm wrong, but didn't you say you wanted to talk to me about something?"

"Yes."

She tapped the face of her watch. "Then get to it, because time is money."

He nodded. "It's about Flower."

River shook her head. "Not this shit again."

"Just hear me out," he sighed. "I think she's lying to you."

She shrugged. "I need more than that."

"I think she's still married. I hate to tell you it but it's true."

"How did you find out?"

"I got ways."

River sat back in her seat. "I don't doubt she's married."

He frowned. "So, you don't have a problem with her being in a relationship with somebody else?"

"I never said that."

He dragged a hand down his face and wiped his hair away. "Then I don't understand, River. At all. Either you care or you don't."

"When her ex-husband put her out on Christmas Eve, it was sudden. I'm sure she's still married because paperwork takes a long time. And — ."

Suddenly five officers barreled into the restaurant and toward the back where she sat. At first River thought they were coming for her, but within seconds they had Tinsley on the floor with his wrists tied behind his back.

Because he was so little, it was an aggressive mean scene.

"Tinsley Adams, you are wanted for questioning in the murder of Benji Cohen." He grabbed his cuffs and slapped them on his tiny wrists.

River jumped off her chair. "What's going on?" Her tallness hung over the crowd. "You don't have to handle him like this!"

"Back up!" One of the officers said, with his hand hovering over the handle of his gun. "Now!"

River raised her hands and did as the officer's said, as she watched her friend be ushered outside by cops. What's worse, for a crime she herself committed.

As the situation ended up outside the bar, she saw the fear in Tinsley's face as he was thrown in the backseat of a squad car like dirty laundry. In that moment she made a decision that no matter what, she would get him out of jail and get the best attorney possible.

Or she would blow the precinct up and get him out.

River was so concerned with her friend, that when she looked up, she was shocked to see Banks standing outside, staring in her direction.

Her cover blown.

PETIT ESTATE

Jersey was sitting on Banks' face as he sucked her clit and fucked her pussy with his tongue. Knowing he enjoyed being smothered, Jersey grinded her juices on his face, until she exploded in his mouth.

When she tried to ease up to take a break, he grabbed her legs and said, "Don't fucking move." His fingertips dug into the flesh of her thighs. "Stay right here. I'm not done."

He continued to lick.

It wasn't a request.

It was a demand.

Although her thighs were weak and her clit vibrated, she knew she would be forced to take the ride to another orgasm. Because when Banks got this way, he could legit eat her out all night.

Jersey didn't know it, but the best way for him to get his mind off of Mason, was by being up under a bad bitch with a clean juicy box.

And Jersey was it.

Because contrary to what Mason believed, Banks believed in his heart that he was done with him, forever.

He even had a plan so that he would never have to see his face ever again.

DASHER'S HOUSE

Mason was sitting on the toilet, with Dasher between his legs sucking his dick. He hadn't called her inside, but when he said he was pissing, she entered without knocking, pushed him down and went to work.

She wanted it nasty.

And so, he obliged.

First, he pissed on her face.

And then, she dropped to her knees fully prepared to finish what she started. At the moment his dick was so deep in her throat, he could see the print of it as he moved in and out.

"Suck this dick, bitch," he said, as he was filled with rage at what happened at the bar. "You wanted this dick, right? Take all of it!"

As she took care of business, his mind roamed.

How dare Banks try to cut him off like he didn't matter.

How dare he cut him off from his kids.

How dare he tried to act, like what they shared never happened.

As Dasher continued to go to work, suddenly Mason closed his eyes. Remembering how good it used to feel when he had Banks in his bed, the dick suck took a different route.

Before long, Dasher's mouth was no longer a mouth. It was a wet pussy that belonged to the one person he still wanted above all else.

In and out he pumped, with his eyes closed, as her mouth grew hotter and wetter. In the end, he pressed a load of creamy vanilla colored cum down her throat. And when she tried to move to come up for air, he grabbed her head closer, until she swallowed every drop.

Only then, did he release his hold and opened his eyes.

For a moment, all was better.

"I love you," she said.

"I know you do."

CHAPTER FOURTEEN

PETIT ESTATE

Rain and thunder clapped around the estate making the mood dark as fuck. Carl was walking up the stairs with a plate of food when he was stopped by Walid. "What you doing?"

"About to have lunch in my bedroom," he winked. "Why? Did you need anything before I retire?"

"I'm bored."

"Your parents are downstairs, aren't they?" He said, referring to Banks and Jersey who were in the kitchen, preparing for the day ahead of them.

"Yes, but I don't like them."

Carl sighed. "Walid, you are going to have to get over your anger. Remember, we talked about that already. I may not be here forever, and you must remember my words!"

"But I—."

He sat the plate of food on the step, lowered his height and plopped down. His long legs flopping outward. Pulling Walid to him he said, "What did I always tell you about your emotions?"

"I don't wanna—."

"What did I tell you?"

"Anger is a sign of the weak."

"Why?"

"Because it means another person controls your destiny."

"And does anybody control your destiny?"

"No." He shook his head slowly from left to right.

"Then stop worrying and stop showing anger to your parents. Things will be fine for you and Ace. And you won't be little forever. I promise."

Flower drove up to the McDonald's drive-thru window and ordered two Happy Meals. When she was done, she pulled up in front of an old brick apartment building.

"I'm outside," she said on her cell phone. "Come help me bring this stuff in. It's raining hard out here."

Within a minute, her husband, Jesse, rushed outside with an umbrella. He kissed her on the lips and slipped back on her tiny wedding ring. "I fucking miss you."

She pulled him back, slipped her tongue deeper into his mouth and said, "I miss you too. So fucking much."

The moment they were in the apartment, she said, "Now, let me see where your ass been. And I bet not smell no whores on you or I'll cut this mothafucka off." His dick was already in her hand.

He was turned all the way on.

Before even hitting the bedroom, she undressed and tore his clothes off at the door. Kneeling down, she placed his long, swollen dick inside her warm mouth and suckled lightly and then harder.

This was perfect, because he had been beating off since she had left, waiting for her return.

The more he moaned, Flower started sucking Jesse's dick more like a pro while jerking him at the same time. She even managed to lick his balls from the back as a tingling sensation ran up his shaft.

Easing on the rug, they ended up in a 69 and so, she began sucking his dick while he played with her pussy at the same time.

"Damn, Jesse, if I would've known you was gonna taste this good I would've been back a long time ago."

Jesse didn't say a word.

He just sat back and enjoyed the experience.

After a while, Flower was freaking him out and so, Jesse couldn't hold back anymore. He couldn't play hard or fake like he didn't want her. The feeling of getting his dick sucked so well drove him insane. And he noticed the more he rubbed her clit, the more she moaned.

Her body moved to the rhythm of his fingers until she couldn't take it anymore either. "Jesse, fuck me please. I want all this dick in my pussy."

Still on the floor, Jesse pulled Flower on top of him while she eagerly grabbed his dick and guided it into her pussy. Like an erotic dancer, she eased up and down the shaft slowly, taking in every inch and adjusting her walls to his size.

Loving the sensation, Flower moved her hips back and forth, rubbing her clit up against Jesse's pubic bone which caused her body to light up with vibrations.

Within minutes, they exploded.

Together.

When they were done, they ate their cold meals in bed and smoked cigarettes. They were puffing so long; the space was full of smoke and their eyes dried out. Placing her head on his chest she inhaled and exhaled.

"You felt so good," she moaned, wrapping her leg around his. "I miss you so fucking much."

"You sure about that?" He stroked her back.

"What you mean?" She looked up at him.

"You not gonna tell me you ain't been fucking her, Flower? You gonna tell me she ain't been eating that pussy."

She rolled her eyes. "Yeah, she eat this shit. But I thought we said we would stick to the plan."

"And what is the plan again? For you to let some dyke suck you while you scream her name? Huh?"

She rolled her eyes. "Jesse, you can't keep doing this."

"Well how the fuck do you expect me to feel?" He shoved her off of him. "You're supposed to be my wife."

She sat up. "I am your wife."

"Well, I can't tell, because you not here!" He was acting like a bitch which was a turn off for the moment.

She sat against the headboard. "Jesse, River is rich. Big rich! That was the entire point of us doing all of this. That's why we came up with our plan." She paused. "I fucking seen it with my own eyes."

"You mean you have access to her money, and you didn't take it already?" He hopped up from the bed, while glaring down at her. "Fuck is you waiting on? Secure the bag!"

"I counted the money she keeps in the house. It's over two hundred thousand dollars. But that's just what she keeps in the house. And that's not even everything."

Now he was calm. "I'm listening."

"So, she has more money hidden somewhere. She doesn't keep it in the crib because she doesn't believe in putting all of her eggs in one basket. At least that's what she told me. But more than that, she knows where

Mason's money is too. She knows about the drops. Sometimes she picks them up, sometimes he does for old time sake. I've heard her speak to him on more than one occasion."

"So, you want me to get my niggas again and—."

"Not yet. Just keep doing what you been doing by harassing the Wales' and the Lou's. We need to keep their anxieties high at all times."

"Why?"

"Because when we steal the money, I don't want River thinking it was me. I don't want her thinking I was involved. Luckily Banks and Mason are already beefing about Ace, so when it's time to bounce it will be easy to cast blame."

"But why would Banks steal money from River? Isn't he rich?"

"Who said it had to be him stealing the money? It could be one of the men he hires. The point is, since they are already at war, we can take the cash and they would never suspect us. And by the time they do, we'll be in Aruba." She giggled. "Now, I know you followed Spacey and hung around his house, but did you do the other thing too?"

"You mean follow Mason?"

"Yes, Jesse."

"We pulled up on him so he could see us. A few times at the hospital, but the one time he got shook is when we pulled up on him at a light. Nigga ran through traffic and almost got hit by a mac truck." He chuckled. "Punk ass nigga."

"See, paranoia is setting in. I give it a few more days and we will be straight."

He grabbed her on the bed and pulled her into his arms. "Why are you so fucking smart?"

She shrugged. "Because I want more."

He frowned. "Fuck that supposed to mean?"

She sighed. "After I got my degree, I didn't realize how much I would have to give up to get the life I wanted. How demanding being a doctor is. And then when the pandemic hit, I didn't feel secure in having to expose myself to that much disease to get paid. I mean how good will that money be if I die from COVID and never get to enjoy it? I realized, I want the lifestyle River gave me, minus River."

"I don't know whether to be happy or fucked up."

"You gotta stop competing with her." She tossed her hands up.

"Who said I was—."

"When we first got together you said there wasn't a female alive who could pull a bitch you wanted."

"It's the truth."

"I thought it was, and that shit turned me on."

"I meant it too."

"I thought you did, and then you changed on me a little. Kept asking me questions about a bitch I left for you."

"Flower—."

"Nah, you gotta listen. I picked you because I want you, nigga. And I want you because you are perfect for me. All I'm asking is that you have one ounce of the swag she does when shit gets tough."

He glared. "Easy on the disrespect."

"No disrespect."

"Sometimes you think just because something is in your head, it needs to be said. You gonna have to watch that shit." He pointed at her.

"Meaning?"

"If you do it around me, you do it around River too. And all it takes is you saying the wrong thing that raises her antennas. Or somebody else's antennas. So, chill on the lip service."

"Nothing will get in the way of my plans."

"Did you hear anything I just said?"

"I did."

"Tell me what I said."

"You said I don't have to say everything that's on my mind. And that I need to chill."

"So, you are listening. Now pay the fuck attention."

"Yes, but I'm telling you that when I say what's on my mind it's only because I'm confident. Confident that she's not on to us. Confident that she is so far in my pussy, that she thinks I can do no wrong."

"Flower—."

"It's true. When the dust settles, Banks and Mason will be at each other's heads, and you and I will be in Aruba, living out our dreams. More than a million dollars richer."

CHAPTER FIFTEEN

PREACH'S HOME

Priscilla, Preach's wife was cooking dinner while talking to her cousin on the phone. With the cell propped up on a stand, she was able to facetime her while chopping onions in preparation for the night's meal.

"Girl, I keep telling you what to eat if you want your pussy to smell fresh." Priscilla giggled. "But you don't listen." She shook her head.

"How on earth can what you eat make your pussy stink?"

"Wait, are you serious?" She asked looking at her via the screen. "You gotta be playing with me."

"Yes, bitch. Not washing it can make it foul but not what you eat."

"You know what, I blame your mother." Priscilla dropped the onions in her stew. "First off you can't be eating seafood every day. Crabs and shrimp on a regular will make your body smell like trash. Plus, you know crabs and lobster are called the cockroaches of the sea. Look it up."

"Whatever, girl." She waved at the screen.

"You keep believing that if you want to."

Her cousin laughed. "Anyway, are we going out the country or not? Because I been shopping nonstop for our vacation."

She sighed and shook her head. "I don't know."

"What changed all of a sudden? Going out of town was ya'lls idea in the first place. Now that me and Rick are with it ya'll missing in action."

"It's not me. It's Preach."

"What's wrong? He sick or something?"

"Nah, just got some problems going on with his boss."

"Girl, he always got something going on with…"

KNOCK! KNOCK! KNOCK!

Priscilla's eyes widened. "Hey, let me hit you back." She wiped her hands on a towel.

"Make sure you call back too! I need to know are we going out of town or nah! I'm sick of waiting on ya'll!"

"I will, now let me go!" She ended the call and rushed to the door.

Once in her living room, she was surprised to see a white face on the security camera. At first, she was scared and then she saw a badge on his hip and wanted to shit herself.

The man looked all kinds of serious.

Immediately her heart rate increased, and she placed her warm hand over her chest to calm down. After all, she was certain that the cop was there due to Natty going missing.

At least she hoped so.

So, it was important that she keep her cool.

With one last deep breath, she pulled the door open and smiled like Mrs. Cleaver. "How can I help you?" She rubbed her hands on her apron like a good little housewife.

"I'm looking for Shawn Park." He pulled out a small pad and flipped through pages. "I believe he goes by the name Preach."

"Uh, yes."

"Is he here?"

"Yes, I mean, no. He lives here but he's not home."

"Can I come in and talk to you for a moment?"

"Uh, yes, sure," she opened the door wider. "I'm just making dinner."

"This won't be long." He walked inside and sat on the sofa.

Trying to appear cool, she flopped in the recliner and crossed her legs. "How can I help you, officer? I mean, is everything alright?"

"Not really. We are looking for a young lady who goes by the name Natty."

The woman lost rhyme and reason. "Oh, I, you, I mean, he, man...I—."

When he saw she unraveled he knew he was on to something. "Are you okay?"

She pointed at the kitchen with her thumb and looked back at him. "Yes, um, it's just that dinner is—."

"Do you know this female?" He said firmly.

"No, I don't."

He leaned in closer, arms to the top of his thighs. "Let me tell you what's going to happen. You are either going to tell me where your husband is, right now, or you will be an accessory to the fact if we find him guilty of a crime. This is not a game. We are very serious. Now where is your husband?"

She swallowed three times before calming down. "He's at one of his properties. I mean, I think he's at one."

"What kind of property?"

"He rehabs homes."

"Okay, do you know which one he's located at right now?" He pulled a pen from his coat pocket along with his tiny pad.

"Yes, I think so." She nodded so much her neck hurt.

He gave her a serious stare. "That's not going to be good enough. I need exact information."

"Uh, yes, I know where he is."

After he recorded the address, she gave him, he made his exit, but not without a stark warning. "I would be leery of calling your husband before we speak to him. It won't bode well for you if the girl turns up murdered, and he's involved." With that he walked out the door.

Not knowing what to do, she quickly called Preach. In a sense she picked a side.

"Baby, I buckled, and I'm so fucking sorry," she cried. "I'm so fucking sorry! Please call me back! Now!"

When she ended the call, she prayed the officer wouldn't get to him before she could reach him first.

After leaving Preach's house, Hercules walked to his car and entered the address Priscilla gave him in the GPS. He was able to personate a cop so easily, not because he did a great job at acting, but mainly because Priscilla knew her husband was guilty of a crime.

And the guilty always buckled under pressure.

With the newfound information in tow, he rushed to the scene.

BANKS' MAYBACH

By T. STYLES

Banks was in his car, on the way to the grocery store to buy a few items Jersey requested for the dinner with his adult children that night. To be honest he wasn't in the mood, but once he got in his car, away from it all, he was glad she suggested he make the run.

It felt good being able to breathe for a moment.

Tapping a button on his steering wheel he attempted to reach the one man he felt could ensure Ace would be okay, by getting the woman who started the drama off the streets.

"Call Preach."

Within seconds, his car dialed Preach's number, and again it went to voicemail. This was frustrating to him for a number of reasons.

For starters, he needed to make sure that once he won custody of Ace, that she wouldn't pop back up in the picture and destroy things again. Which would result in Ace being taken. He wasn't even sure what her purpose was in the first place.

And it was also the fact that he gave Preach a lot of money to find Carmen. Because when it came to finding her, Banks spared no expense. He would've gotten more professionals involved but didn't want the dirt of his past as a drug dealer being kicked up in the process.

Was it possible that Preach used him?

He decided to leave a message. "Preach, I don't know where you are, but I hope you aren't fucking with me. It wouldn't be good for your health." He paused. "Call me. A.S.A.P."

After ending the call, he continued to the grocery store, but Preach was definitely heavy on his mind.

CHAPTER SIXTEEN

MASON'S MERCEDES TRUCK

Mason and Dasher were driving down the street, when he looked over at her before focusing back on the road. She really was a beauty, and at the same time, he never connected with her on an emotional level.

Something she wanted sincerely.

"What?" She smiled.

"Can you be with a nigga like me for the rest of your life?" He steered the car down the road.

Her eyes widened. "You sound crazy."

He frowned. "How you figure?"

"Mason, there is nothing, or nobody I want more in the world than you." She positioned her body to look directly at him. "Everything that I have ever done since we've been together, has been because I want you." She placed her hand over her heart. "Don't you know that?"

"Why?" He shrugged.

"Where do I start?"

"Wherever you want."

"For starters, I'm so fucking attracted to you, baby. Just looking at you, my panties are slick right now."

She said it in a way that he never heard anybody say it before. If nothing else, he felt the passion in the words and for some reason his dick jumped.

"What else?"

"I feel safe when I'm around you. I feel like, like, I can do anything. Like the sky's the limit and it's such a turn on."

He nodded. "That's deep."

"It's deep and true. And the sex." She moaned. "I swear I'm not making this up, but I never had a man who sinks into me the way you do. And I'm addicted to it, Mason. I want more of it. And I love you for it."

If she was lying, he couldn't spot the lie. "How do I know I can trust what you say?"

She took a deep breath. "I want to tell you something, but I don't want you to be mad after I tell you this."

He glared. "I can't make no promises."

"Then I won't tell you. Because the purpose of what I'm about to say, is not because I want to bring us further apart, but because I want to bring us closer together. And I think now is the time."

He nodded.

Everything in him wanted to fight her conditions, but he was tired of the struggle. If he was going to take the next step, he needed to know everything.

Even the dark things.

"Okay." He wiped a hand down his face and leaned to the side as he continued to drive. "I promise I won't get angry."

"I stole your sperm, out of the condom after we fucked, to get pregnant."

Silence.

"Mason? Did you hear me?" She said with wide eyes. "And are you mad?"

"Why did you do that?"

"Because I was willing to do whatever I could, to keep you in my life. And I knew this body could make a baby you would be proud of. I knew Bolt would be beautiful. And he was even more. So, when you say you don't believe I want you more than anything, how many women do you know will go to those lengths?"

He couldn't name one.

And he also did basically the same thing with Banks and Jersey which resulted in the Twins.

So, who was he to point the finger?

"And I'm also willing to play the backseat, to who you really want." She looked down.

"Fuck are you talking about?" He parked at the location they were going.

"I know who you really desire, and I am very confident that I can love you harder than he can. And I will love you how you deserve to be treated. If you want me on my knees, then that's where I'll remain until you lift me up."

He started to lie and say she was wrong.

But why?

Everybody knew how he felt about Banks, and so he decided to stay mum.

"I want you to be my wife. But I wanna do this quick. No ceremony. Just us applying for our license and getting married in a week. I want to have a mother for my younger children, including Ace and Walid. Are you with it?"

Her eyes appeared to stretch over her entire face as she trembled. "Yes, Mason!" She reached over and snatched his neck, while crying heavily. "Yes, I will marry you! Please don't change your mind. I'm begging you."

When they released, he said, "Nah, I want this. Like I said, for more reasons than one."

"Hey, so, I know you gotta go handle business." She rubbed his chest. "But do you mind if I taste you right quick?"

His dick thumped as he looked into her eyes. She just finished sucking him off, but it was as if she couldn't get enough. "Oh yeah?"

She rubbed his dick and undid his jeans. "Yeah."

Before he could dispute, Dasher had removed his stick and placed him firmly into her mouth. Her tongue felt like a hot oven, and he was sure it wouldn't last long.

"Piss in my mouth," she said, as she continued to suck, spit dripping everywhere.

"You wanna taste this shit?"

"Please," she begged. "I wanna taste it all."

Holding the back of her head, Mason pushed repeatedly into her throat until he could feel himself swelling.

"Suck that shit," he directed, as she Houdinied his dick and within seconds, he exploded into her mouth.

Raising her head, she opened her jaw and showed him that she swallowed every drop.

"See you when you get back."

"Damn, girl," he sighed. "Let me hurry up right quick."

She giggled.

And as he eased out of the car and walked around the back of one of his houses, he thought about what he just did.

Propose marriage.

No, he wasn't in love with Dasher.

And at the same time, his father told him to always marry someone who loves you more than you love them, and Dasher was definitely that person. But he was also trying to build a family for the fight he was in for with the Twins.

In his mind things would look better if he had a wife to go along with having the perfect life.

The moment he bent the corner and walked behind one of his properties, to get his money, he felt like something was off. Before they could catch him, he wiggled under the crawl space.

The earth against Mason Louisville's belly was damp and smelled of the foulness given to the air, when something living died.

And yet there he lie, on the ground, afraid that after everything he had done in life, some good, more bad, this would be his final moment on earth.

So, he took in what would inevitably be his coffin.

The coolness of the air.

The thump of his heart.

And the silent breathing of a predator who was nearby.

Before long, he could hear footsteps in the distance, and still, if he planned correctly, maybe the grim reaper would not find him. Besides, he was well hidden. And only the most vicious of snipers or hired killers would have thought to look for him beneath the house.

He could stay there in perfect darkness all night if need be.

And then something happened.

Something that on the scale of things, may not have seemed so bad.

Due to a few kicks of his boot, he had unraveled a bed of red fire ants, which took to crawling up his legs, and gnawing at the flesh of his ankles. To say it was painful was an understatement. Their tiny bodies worked diligently up his thighs, moving viciously toward his crotch area.

As if their primary focus was to get him to give up his position.

And yet, he had to take the pain.

He had to take the heat.

For if he did not, the agony of bullets would far outweigh the sting of their bites.

And so, he remained, hoping Mrs. Death would be denied, and pass him over once more.

When out of the corner of his eyes, he saw the boots of a man, he whipped out his gun and shot him in the ankle.

Quickly he wiggled out of the crawl space and shot the man in his leg as he attempted to run. When he tried to hop off, Mason shot him again in the other leg, before kicking the gun he was holding out of his hand when he fell.

"Who the fuck are you?" Mason asked standing over top of him, still feeling the stings of the ants on his skin. "And why you trying to kill me?"

"I was just trying to see what was in this house. I wasn't—."

"Don't lie to me! You were following me! And I want to know why! Who are you? And don't lie to me!"

"My name is Seedy."

"What the fuck you want with me?"

"Banks sent me."

Mason's heart dropped in his shoes. The pain he felt was too hard to describe. His dearest friend, really wanted him gone.

"What you mean he sent you?"

"He sent me to kill you," he continued. "I been following you for weeks. I'm sorry. I didn't—."

BOOM!

BOOM!

Mason heard enough, and so he fired in his chest, killing him instantly. Walking away from the corpse, after calling Banks' phone and not getting an answer, he called Jersey next.

"What, Mason?"

"Where is Banks?"

"He's not here, why?"

Mason smiled. "So, he wants war huh?"

"Fuck are you talking about this time? You always talking shit."

"Tell your man that he won't know the time or the hour, but I'm coming for him. That's on my life!"

MINNESOTA'S ESTATE

Minnesota was getting ready for dinner with her family when Zercy walked up behind her and looked at her in the mirror.

"I really am sorry, Minnesota." He kissed her cheek. "About my sisters."

She turned around and looked up at him. "I wish I understood what possessed you to tell your sisters about me and my brother in the first place. I wish I could understand but it misses me. You should've seen how Joey looked at me. I was so, so ashamed."

"I don't know what got into me."

"Zercy, that's not fucking good enough." She glared.

He looked down and then walked away, before flopping on the edge of the bed. "That's all I can give you for now."

For some reason, Minnesota looked at him closely and it was as if the lights were turned on in her mind. The actions he claimed were so out of personality for him. "You didn't tell them, did you?"

He raised his head slowly and their eyes met. "No."

"Why did you make me believe it then?"

"They bugged my phone. One of those voice and phone trackers they sell everywhere since the pandemic. I kept my phone on me at all times, and when the case cracked, I found the tracker inside. It was a week after me and you got together, and you told me about Spacey. They must've been listening in."

She sat next to him on the bed. "Zercy, your sisters are dangerous. You have to do something about them."

"I will."

"You have no choice. With them in the picture, I don't know if we'll get married. Because I'm legit in fear for my life." She swallowed. "Zercy, is there anything else you haven't told me?"

His eyes said yes.

"Please tell me now."

"I have a brother. A twin brother that I wasn't raised with. Not identical."

She frowned. "What's his name?"

"My parents had an infinity for Z names. His name Zantonio. But he goes by Z."

Having recognized the moniker, Minnesota felt sick to her stomach once again.

The lies of it all.

Truce 3: Sins of The Fathers

CHAPTER SEVENTEEN

PETIT ESTATE

The dinner table at the Petit mansion was flooded with an array of food. Italian cuisine was the theme for the evening. And Jersey, with the help of hired caterers, went all out to make the night special.

In attendance were Banks, Jersey, Spacey, Minnesota, Shay and Joey. Despite the tension in the months prior, everyone did their level best to make the mood light, desperately hoping that things would get better for the Wales gang.

There was one problem.

Most wanted to know if Banks had forgiven them for their plays in the Blaire ordeal with Mason, and he had yet to give them an answer.

Banks looked smooth in his black button-down shirt and designer blue jeans. His hair was cut just long enough for a few curls to pop through the short mane.

And he looked fucking good.

When the food was served and eaten, Banks said, "I want to talk to you all now." Banks sipped his wine and looked upon each face. "About something that's very serious." He placed down his glass.

Everyone put down their forks and gave him their undivided.

"We've been through a lot over the past few months." Banks said in a low voice. "And I'm sorry about my part in all of it."

"Pops, it's not your fault," Shay said.

"She's right. I wish like hell I could take back everything," Minnesota said, desperately trying not to cry.

"Yeah, dad, we should've been honest with you from the gate," Spacey nodded. "I'm just happy you gave us this chance to be here tonight. And it will never, ever happen again."

"I feel the same too, Pops," Joey said, pleased his siblings were trying to make things smooth. "Family over everything."

Banks nodded. "I wish I can remember who Banks was as a man. Because I can see in your eyes, all of you, how much he means to you when you look at me. All I can say, is that I didn't feel myself until I got back in his skin. For years, I felt disconnected when I lived in this house. I felt like a fraud in my clothes and while wearing makeup. But when I reconnected with some of Banks' memories, I felt like things were coming together."

Jersey squeezed his hand.

"But my memory has not returned fully. And so, I don't remember you in the way I want to, and I don't know if that will ever change."

They all got the answer to another one of their questions.

He didn't have all of his memories back.

Shay looked down and Minnesota rubbed her back.

"But I do know that until this moment, until this very night, I didn't realize the other piece missing in my life. Just being here with all of you together, out of the Louisville household, I see clearer. This is what I miss. This is what I need. La Familia."

Shay looked down, feeling mostly relieved. "Does this mean you will forgive everybody. Even Mason?"

He glared. "Nothing with Mason and I will ever be the same." After hearing the threat Jersey said he sent earlier that night, he was definitely done with him.

"But the two of you have been friends for so long," Shay begged. "And I know you don't remember him, but both of you were so close. And—."

"If he was a real friend, he would've told me the truth about who I was. And as far as I'm concerned, he's dead to me."

"Pops—."

"I understand your need to defend him," Banks said raising his hand which cut Shay off. "But there is nothing you can say that will convince me to change my mind. I also get your loyalty to the Louisville family. After all, you're married to one. But there will come a time when you'll have to choose. It's either the Wales' or the Lou's. But it can't be both. I won't ask you to make a decision now. You have a few days."

Everyone looked at her and nodded in agreement.

River was right.

"Anyway, I want you all to know that I will be taking the Twins and Blakeslee. We all are moving out of the country by the beginning of next year. Jersey as well. I bought a beautiful piece of property in Belize."

What struck everyone was not that he was moving, but that the purchasing of islands was just so fucking Banks Wales.

"Why are you leaving?" Spacey asked. "Are you in trouble?"

"I can't tell you why exactly I'm leaving. To be honest I don't know. All I can say is just like being in this skin, with this hair and these clothes feels right, being overseas feels right too. It's like, I see myself flying above the sky, and never coming back. And it's the only thing I have to look forward to. I hear Minnesota is getting married. Maybe you can have your wedding there."

She smiled. "Maybe."

And the Wales children looked at one another.

"And whoever wants to come with me, and Jersey are free to do so."

A sudden gasp filled the room.

That was the statement a few were looking for because they wanted to be where he was.

"If you wish to leave with me, I promise you this, I will make a life for you all that you cannot imagine. You will want for nothing. You will have everything. And it will be my desire to make sure that above all else, you have peace."

The wheels in a lot of their minds began to churn.

Could they bounce?

Would they bounce?

"But, if you leave with me, there is no coming back. I don't want anyone knowing where we are. Especially not Mason."

While everyone sat around the table and talked within the Petit Estate, Spacey walked outside to smoke a cigarette, a habit he picked up not too long ago.

He was really considering what his father said and wondering what a life would look like overseas. Could he live in another country for the rest of his life? And more than it all, would he take his son Riot along for the journey?

The door opened and his brother slid out.

Knowing they were beefing, Spacey was about to go inside when Joey said, "Don't do that, man."

"Do what?"

"Leave. We gotta talk."

He sighed. "About what?"

"I'm not understanding what happened between you and Minnesota. And because I don't understand I'm having a hard time sleeping at night. Like, this shit is really fucking with my mind."

Spacey knew there was no point in avoiding him, especially if they both made a decision to go to Belize. So, it was best to come clean.

"Joey, you will never understand. All I can say is that we thought we were going to die. We were held hostage, in an attic for years. All we had was each other and so we fell in love."

Joey's stomach churned and he wanted to throw the fuck up. "It just doesn't make any sense. Fuck! No sense at all!"

"I know, but I also thought we weren't blood related when we first made love. And I know she still loves me now."

"Do me a favor, and never say *make love* again when you talking about our little sister." He pointed at him.

Spacey rolled his eyes. "Do you want the truth or not?"

Joey sighed. "How the fuck you ain't know ya'll were related?"

"Because it was never clear. When Pops explained everything to you about how we were born, I wasn't there. And Minnie wasn't either. You know what, it doesn't matter, man. It happened and I wish I could take it back."

"That some nasty ass—."

"Joey, please." Spacey said waving the air. "It won't change anything. Definitely not the past. And I hope at one time you will forgive me. At the very least, try to forget. Because it wasn't about you. You weren't there. And you will never understand."

Joey sighed being done with it all. "What are you going to do?"

"With Minnesota?"

"Nah, man," he said wiping the air, still grossed out about their relationship. "Are you going to Belize?"

"Are you?"

Joey nodded with all certainty. "To me, going with him is like taking it back to the beginning. When he wanted to get us away to Wales Island before the war kicked off. Since Pops was a kid he always wanted to live on an island. And going this time, in this way, feels poetic. Besides, he sold Strong Curls so he's richer than ever. Worth billions."

"I heard. Saw it on the news this morning."

"So, you going or not?"

Spacey sighed. "I don't know. It's a lot to consider."

"I would say this, unless you love everything about living here, don't miss out on the opportunity for us to be family again. Bring Riot and start all over. You'll never, ever get a chance like this again. Because once we leave, we'll vanish forever. Like we never existed."

CHAPTER EIGHTEEN

Hercules was driving on the way to the address Priscilla told him Preach would be located in silence. As he drove down the street, he thought about his life. He thought about his mother and for one moment, he blamed her for all of his troubles.

Besides, had she not hunted Banks down, and at the very least, had she not tried to change him into being what he wasn't, a female, maybe she would be alive today. Maybe the virus wouldn't have gotten into her lungs, altering her body and then taking her life.

Maybe her death was karma.

Parking in front of the house, Hercules was surprised to see Preach sitting on the porch smoking a cigarette.

Exiting his car, Hercules sat next to him, before looking over at him once. "It's a nice night. Thought it would be cooler, but this day almost feels like fall."

Preach nodded. "Church."

"Got another cigarette?"

Preach reached into his coat pocket and handed him one.

Hercules put it between his lips and said, "I need a light."

Preach tossed the matches in his lap.

After firing up, Hercules inhaled and allowed smoke to pillow out into the air. "Where is she, man?"

"I don't know what you talking about."

"But you do know exactly what I'm talking about."

Preach shook his head. "I would prefer if you gonna step to me, that you would at least be real. Respect my time, and I'll respect yours."

"I know you know what I'm talking about, because for starters, you never asked who I was."

"I kept eyes on you for a long time when you and your family were stalking Banks, before the brain injury.

So of course, I know who you are. Even if you didn't know me."

Hercules nodded. "Fair enough. So, let me do it like this. You took her from in front of my house."

"Who?"

"Natty."

Preach was going to lie, but after hearing him state facts, it meant he knew more than he let on. "She came with me willingly."

"Is that why you had your friend come back for her car? Because something sounds off."

He looked over at him. "What do you want from me?"

"I want to know where you put the mother of my child."

"Maybe you should leave."

"Let me make myself clear, I'm not going anywhere until you tell me where Natty is. I'm not a joke. I don't play games with —."

BANG!

Upon catching the bullet, the cigarette dropped from his lips and fell to the ground.

Preach had shot him in the side, after having the gun aimed on him the moment his buns touched the steps.

Standing up he shot him again in the chest and watched him topple to the ground. "You should not have come here."

He shot him once more in the belly.

Looking around, he stepped over his body and jumped into his car. The moment he did, his phone rang and he answered. "Preach, where have you been?" The voice said calmly. "I'm tired of waiting."

"Banks?"

"Don't Banks me! Have you found Carmen or not? And why have you been dodging my calls?"

"Banks, I'm sorry, man. I really did try my best to find her. I tried my best to do what was right, but now things are out of hand and I can't stay here anymore."

"What does that mean?"

"It means that I was always loyal to you, despite how things may look. And I hope one day you get the memory of who I was back in the day. And who my father was too. Most of all, I hope you believe I tried."

"Preach, I—."

After hanging up on Banks, he called his wife and said, "He's gone. I'ma let Michigan live though."

"Are you sure?"

"I shot him three times so yes, I'm fucking sure he's dead. I'm sure about Michigan too." He looked at his body once more and pulled away from the scene. "But I need you to listen to me."

"O...okay, okay."

"I need you to go to the house I was telling you about, across from the tree that blooms yellow in spring. There is a slat next to fake roses planted in a weird way. When you walk up on them, you'll see they aren't real.

Dig in the ground, it won't be too deep, and get our money."

"I'm scared, Preach."

"I know, baby, and I'm sorry, but we don't have any choice. We have to leave everything behind and this time forever."

"But what about my businesses and — ."

"I just killed two people! One by accident, the other on purpose. Both are connected to one person and that person is me. Now do you wanna be with me or not?"

"Of course, I do!"

"Then waste no more time! Do what the fuck I'm telling you! Now! Secure the bag."

"Okay," she cried. "Okay."

"I love you, Priscilla. I'll meet you at the house. Bye."

CHAPTER NINETEEN

Concerned she would get snatched up at any moment as the real culprit of Benji's murder, River's head was on a swivel outside the police department as she waited for Tinsley to be released.

She contacted the best criminal defense attorney her money could buy and sent him in to rescue her friend.

An hour later, they walked out, and Tinsley had a sad expression covering his face. His wig was off, but his face was still beat.

Wanting to greet him, River rushed out to help. Her 6-foot frame towered over his 5'2 frame.

As if he was both injured and fragile, she slowly walked him to the passenger seat. Once he was securely inside, she got in and pulled off.

"What...what happened?" She asked softly.

"A lot." He sighed. "In the end they were threatening charging me with murder, because they found his DNA and blood in my house. On the living room floor. But I didn't do it. I promise."

"I know you didn't." River looked away, unable to contain her guilt.

She knew he didn't do it because she had killed his ass.

When she murdered the man, it was to protect Tinsley. Now she was realizing she put him directly into harm's way.

"Is there anything I can do?" She paused. "Because I won't let them put this on you."

"I'm grateful you got me a lawyer. He was able to buy me some time since they haven't officially charged me, but he's not sure how long they will wait." He looked down.

River looked away from Tinsley in shame.

He shrugged. "Whatever is supposed to happen will happen, River. And I don't want you involved. Besides,

I just found out there may be an opportunity to escape it all with Banks. Maybe I will take it."

She cleared her throat, not knowing what he meant or even caring about Banks Wales. "Hungry?"

"No," he said looking down. "I just wanna go home."

For a second, they drove in silence until River pulled up at Tinsley's favorite fried chicken carryout spot. Once parked she said, "What you want? The usual?"

He looked over at the restaurant, then at her and said, "I can't stand you." A smile covered his face.

She winked and said, "The thing is, you love me though." She touched his leg. "And don't fake like I don't know you. I'ma get your favorite."

"Thank you. I want honey biscuits too."

"You know I knew that already."

Fifteen minutes later, they were sitting in the parking lot eating, as silence hung between them heavily.

"Why do they hate us?" Tinsley finally said softly.

"What you talking about?" River tore into the meat.

"Gay people. Or people who don't look like them. Why do they hate us so much?" The chicken he was eating dropped in the carton in his lap.

River grabbed a napkin and wiped her mouth. "I don't know. I wish I did, Tin but I don't and to be honest, I don't give a fuck for real for real."

"They taunted me in there, snatched my wig off and yelled things to me that made me, made me not wanna live."

River was heated upon hearing what he went through. "Put it back on."

"I don't want to."

"Tin, put the fucking wig back on." She said firmer. "Now."

He put it on his head, and then fingered it into position. Next, she opened her glove compartment, grabbed more napkins and wiped the running makeup off his face. "You look beautiful. And you're still standing. It means you won. Fuck them."

He smiled.

"I'm so sorry this happened to you. But I'm here."

He looked up at her with his eyes filled with tears. "All I wanna do, all I wanna do is be me. I don't want anybody to change into me. All I wanna do is be me. Why won't they let us?"

River reached over and for a second they embraced. When they separated and she saw his mascara running down his cheeks again, she grabbed a napkin and wiped his face once more.

"Listen, we can't waste time trying to figure them out. Because guess what, it won't change who we are. We still gonna love who we want. And we still gonna fuck who we want."

He nodded. "It still hurts."

She nodded and started driving. "It gets better. How did Banks know you were here?"

He sighed. "I called him. He would've come, but he's having his family over for dinner tonight. And I didn't want to ruin it."

River laughed once.

"What's funny?"

She shook her head. "That dude is something else."

"Meaning?"

"Does he have memory loss or not? Because one moment he pretends he doesn't know what's going on and the next...the next...he's having dinner with mothafuckas he claims he doesn't fuck with."

"River, what's wrong? Why does it sound like you have it in for him?"

River thought about her promise to Flower to keep what she told him a secret and bit her tongue.

Yes, she wanted to say what was on her mind. But she also knew talking to Tinsley about her issues with Banks wouldn't change anything.

So why do it at all?

"If it came down to choosing him or me, who would you choose?" River asked seriously.

"You talking about Banks?"

"Who else?" River shrugged.

"I hate when we talk about things like this."

"Why? If you and I are ever gonna have a relationship a little bit like we had in the past, we have to deal with our shit right now."

"Okay, do you really wanna deal?" He said throwing his hands up.

"Yes! I asked didn't I?"

"River, you hurt me when you cut me off. You hurt me because you didn't even try to put yourself in my shoes."

"Fuck is you talking about?"

"You see?" Tinsley said pointing at her. "You so dead set on my trusting Mason, just because you knew him first, that you never tried to understand what I went through after hearing he wanted me dead! With my own ears!" Tears rolled down his cheeks. "Of course, I wanted to trust you, but I was scared! Mason may love you, but he doesn't give a fuck about me!"

River looked away.

He was speaking facts.

"What do you have to say about that, River?" He cried, while wiping his tears away roughly. "Tell me something."

She sighed. "I'm sorry."

He was shocked that she gave in so easily. Because she was tough to crack. "Wait, did you just say you're, you're sorry?"

She looked over at him once and focused back on the road. "I won't say it again."

He sniffled and wiped some more tears away. "Thank you. I know that was hard since you mean and all."

She shrugged as she pulled into the Four Seasons hotel parking lot. "Yeah, it was. And I can't say it will happen again."

He frowned. "What are we doing here?"

"You gotta get cleaned up and I don't want you going back to Banks' crib tonight." She handed her keys over to the valet driver. "Since he having a party and all. Fake ass nigga."

"I said dinner." He shook his head. "Not party."

"Yeah, well, whatever."

Twenty minutes later they were in a room. River made sure he had all the amenities to be comfortable. After bugging the hell out of room service and seeing that all his needs were met, she said, "Go take a shower."

"Will you be here when I get out?" He asked with hopeful eyes.

She nodded yes.

Relieved, Tinsley dipped into the bathroom and removed the wig. Turning on the hot water, he eased inside, he allowed it to beat all over his body, as he cried a bit more. As the tears poured, he felt as if everything was going out of control and he desperately wanted things to get better.

But how?

Or when?

When he got out of the shower, dried off and wrapped the soft white robe around his body, he almost felt like himself.

When he put the wig back on, and fingered it cute, he felt even better.

Exiting the bathroom, he sat on the edge of the bed, next to her and said, "You."

"You what?" She shrugged.

"If it comes down to it, I will choose you over Banks. Every time."

She nodded. "You just saying that."

"I swear on what's left of my life, it would be you, River. I would choose you over everybody. Can you say the same?"

She was silent a bit longer. But when she was ready to speak, her words were gospel. "Let me be clear, Mason will never come in between us again. Ever."

Tinsley got in bed, under the sheets and looked at River. "You mind rocking me to sleep? How you used to do when we lived together."

"You're such a baby."

"I know but I need you right now."

"I gotta go home to Flower and —."

"Please, River. I won't keep you all night." He tossed the sheets back for her to ease behind him.

River sighed, looked at how adorable he was and shook her head. "We ain't been cool but for one day and already you getting your way." She removed her top shirt and pants and folded them on the bed before slipping behind Tinsley in a spoon fashion. She was wearing only boxer briefs and a wife beater. "You spoiled as fuck."

"Thank you," Tinsley said.

"Just go to sleep." She squeezed him tightly and pulled him closer as a man would his bitch. The warmth of her breath caressed his neck and made him feel at home.

"Don't leave me until I'm sleep." He nestled closer to her, feeling safe in her arms.

"I won't. I promise."

Tinsley moved into her again, and for some reason, something strange happened. The curve of his small body aroused her in some way.

But why?

She had never, ever been attracted to a man or anything masculine in her life.

But was Tinsley really a man?

He certainly wasn't masculine.

"What you doing?" River raised her head. "Why you moving into me like that?"

"Close your eyes, River. Please. Just try. I'm begging you to try."

"Try what?" She snapped. "Fuck is you even talking about?"

"Just, close your eyes and touch me." Tinsley was on the verge of crying. "You don't know how much I need this."

"Fuck no, we can't be…"

"I may get locked up forever in a couple of days. This moment may be all I have. Please don't take it from me because I don't fit the picture."

With the guilt of the crime she committed firmly on her back, she closed her eyes. And he took her hand softly.

First, he ran it along the side of his stomach, and then his legs. He felt as soft as any woman she'd been with in the past and so she was surprised. He even guided her hand along the curves of his ass, and still, she could not tell the difference.

But Tinsley obviously wanted more.

Not being able to take it much longer, he guided her hand to his stiffness. Which was small, considering.

"What are you doing?" River breathed.

"Just try…please."

At first, he guided her motions forcefully.

But suddenly it was River who stroked him softly, while nestling her nose into the back of his neck. And before long he moaned. The sound coming from him was as light as a feather, feminine and erotic.

River felt herself heating up, and if she was strapped, she would've fucked him on site.

No questions asked.

Instead, she stroked him slowly at first and then faster, until he exploded on her hand. His warm cream running between her fingertips.

His heavy breaths softening into a light hum.

And as quickly as it happened, guilt settled between the friends and it was over.

She stood up and got dressed, as he pulled the covers over his body. "I'm sorry, River."

"I gotta go."

He knew she was done after what happened because she wouldn't even look his way.

But River shocked him.

Instead of leaving without words, she walked over to him, kissed him on the cheek and said, "I gotta make a few runs, but I'll be back to scoop you up and take you back to Banks' in the morning." Without waiting on his response, she walked out the door.

And he smiled.

CHAPTER TWENTY

LOUISVILLE ESTATE

Shay stood over Derrick and looked at him sideways in their bedroom as he did sit ups on the floor. After Banks' offer to go to Belize, she was wondering if staying in a marriage she was suspicious of was worth giving up an opportunity of a lifetime.

She didn't even tell him what Banks said.

"Derrick..." she mumbled softly as he continued to sit up.

"Yeah..."

"Can you see spending the rest of your life with me?"

He looked up at her and did another sit up. "Fuck yeah."

"I'm serious. Can you see spending forever with me? Whatever that may mean?"

He grabbed the towel on the floor and wiped his face. "Before I get into all that, you still gonna give me some head in the shower, right? Because I been thinking about it all night since you offered."

"Derrick!"

"Yes!"

"Yes, what?" She said crossing her arms.

"Yes, I can see spending forever with you. I mean don't get me wrong, things won't be perfect always. But I don't wanna be with no one else but you."

She nodded. "You sure? Because you haven't been texting lately, but I don't know if you broke up with your fake girl or..."

"You always wanna fight."

"I'm serious. And I'm not fighting nobody. I just wanna feel safe."

He got up and pulled her into his arms, sweat and all. "What is it?"

"If I did something that would make me happy and it didn't include you, how would you feel?"

He laughed and let her go. "It depends."

"On what?"

"Like if you were eating ice cream without sharing and shit like that, I would be cool."

She sat on the edge of the bed. "Let's say it *was* ice cream, and I ate it without you, and didn't even offer you any despite you possibly wanting some, would you hate me if it made me happy? I mean, really, really happy."

"Let me put it like this, as long as it makes you happy, and especially if it makes you *really* happy, I want you to do it, even if it doesn't include me." He slapped her on the ass and said, "Now let me jump in the shower. And don't take too long. I'm trying to tap them tonsils."

As he disappeared into their bathroom, she was undressing when she got a phone call.

Rushing to grab it, she was shocked to see it was Minnesota on the other line. "Hey, what's up?"

"Shay!" She said crying hard.

"What's wrong?"

"They found Natty! She's dead!"

Shay was lying in her bed, holding her son who was asleep when she received yet another call that rocked her world. She couldn't say she was sad, but she wasn't happy either about the woman dying she was sure her husband was fucking.

After learning about Natty, Derrick suddenly had to leave out to go on a liquor run, since Mason preferred it not be in the house.

Why was he so crushed by Natty's death?

When her phone rang again, she sat up in bed when she saw Flower's number. "Hello."

"Hey, girl. You good?"

"Yeah, my sister just called and said her friend was killed."

"I didn't know you had a sister."

She frowned. "Yes, I do. Minnesota Wales."

"Oh." She said sarcastically.

"What?"

"Just didn't know ya'll were so close and everything. But maybe it's good that I'm calling after all."

"Why you say that?"

"I have it on good authority that Mason is placing a hit on Banks' head. The only reason I'm telling you is because we are the black sheep in the family, and I didn't know what else to do."

"What?" She said popping up in bed, almost waking Patrick. "A hit? Why do you say that?"

"I overheard River talking to him. And like I said, the only reason I'm telling you is because we close. But this will be the last time I tell you anything. If something pops off, you're on your own. And if you do decide to tell Banks, I would do it in a roundabout way and don't mention me. Just, just be careful. Okay?"

CHAPTER TWENTY-ONE

B anks and Mason sat in the psychiatrist's office alone, as the doctor made one last attempt to decide Ace's fate. Both of the men barely looked at one another, and it was obvious that the time of being good friends was a thing of the past.

Besides, Shay spoke to Banks about what she heard last night, without telling who told her the information, that his life was in danger.

So now he was on edge.

And Mason, after being hunted down behind one of his properties, also felt the days of being friends were long gone.

"I appreciate you two coming alone today, because I believe it will help me make my final assessment, which will later be given to Ace's social worker." He sighed. "So, who would like to begin today?"

"I will," Banks said.

He nodded, believing like always he would get nowhere. "Go ahead."

"My father has been coming to me in memories lately. I don't remember a lot, but I remember his energy. He was a very, very nervous man. Always on edge. And I can remember, without remembering, being afraid. I can remember wanting to escape. And I can feel the difference of the man I am today, as opposed to the man he was back then."

"That's a lot of progress." Dr. Porter was surprised.

"It's *some* progress. For me anyway." Banks corrected him. "I also remember the feeling of my mother. Of her being anxious, uneasy and on edge." He shook his head. "Bringing a kid up in that much drama is hard. And I vow, that when Ace is given back to me, all of his days, every last one of them will be in peace in paradise."

"Thank you, Mr. Wales."

Banks nodded. "I won't let the sins of my father visit themselves on me anymore, or my sons."

"I have some memories too," Mason said sitting back in his chair.

The doctor nodded very surprised. "I'm listening."

"I remember the feeling I had after learning that my father was killed by his father." He looked over at Banks and back at the doctor. "I remember being made fatherless when all my dad did was try to help his father feed him." He looked over at Banks again. "And it makes me wonder."

Banks and Mason stared at each other, both with evil in their eyes.

"It makes me wonder what would have happened if my father was smarter. Saw the threat in advance and acted faster. It makes me wonder if he would be alive today."

The psychiatrist moved uneasily, once again feeling the tension between two powerful men.

"But I won't make that mistake." He said continuously looking at Banks. "Because I won't let the sins of my father visit themselves on me, or *my* boys either."

"I'll give my decision to Ace's social worker. She will be in contact very soon, along with CPS. Be ready."

While the two traded death stares, the psychiatrist gave updates on what would potentially happen next with Ace. He knew what he was going to recommend, even if he didn't tell them.

But it was obvious at that moment, that things would never be the same.

MINNESOTA'S ESTATE

It was a cool January day as Minnesota sat in her backyard overlooking her property. She was thinking about her life. A lot was involved. Starting with making a decision on whether or not to leave with her father to Belize, or to stay put in Maryland with Zercy.

And at the same time, she wasn't feeling them siblings at all.

"I bought you some hot chocolate," he said, extending a cup in her direction. "Put a little whipped cream on it and everything the way you like."

She pulled the drawstrings of her robe closed and looked out at her land. "Nah. I'm good."

"Still not talking to me, huh?" He took a seat in the lawn chair next to her. "Because we can't stay like this forever."

Silence.

"Minnesota, don't do this to us. Don't do this to me, baby. I mean, I know I was wrong but—."

"You lied to me." She looked at him square on. "You've been lying to me for a while, and I'm tired of it."

"I didn't lie to you."

"What do you call it then?" She threw her hand in the air. "I find out you related to the friend of a man I used to fuck with. How does that supposed to make me feel?"

"My brother doesn't want anything from you." He sat the cup on the table.

"How do you know? I mean, seriously. How do you know he didn't use the triplets to get to me, since Myrio is gone? And they think I had something to do with it." She paused. "Mind you I haven't seen Myrio in I don't know how long. He could be anywhere."

Actually, he was dead.

And since she was the one who pulled the trigger only for Mason to get rid of the body, it was a fact that he was never coming back.

"I'll talk to them, baby. I'll make it known that all of the lies and drama have to stop now."

"You're the strongest man I know. And at the same time, you are the weakest nigga I've ever met in my life."

"Why would you say some shit like that to me?"

"The truth hurts."

"Minnie, baby…"

She raised her hand. "I'm done with the talking, Zercy. Something is up with ya'll niggas. I can feel it in my soul."

"I'm not letting you go, Minnesota. Not over a mistake."

"One of two things is happening. Either you're just like them and trying to destroy me. Or you're trying to protect them. In either scenario, I'm not feeling it, Zercy because if you gonna be with me, I'm gonna be first. I'm a Wales. First is a must. Decide." She got up, removed the ring and tossed it in his lap. "Be out of my house within the hour." She walked away.

LOUISVILLE ESTATE

Shay was in bed with Derrick, listening to him snore to the Gods. When she was certain he wasn't waking anytime soon, she rolled over and crept out of bed.

There…on the nightstand on his side of the room, was the object of her attention. And she was going to get that phone so help her God.

With every snore, she moved closer to the table until the device was within her paws.

"Got you, nigga," she said to herself.

It didn't take long and after a few strokes, she was inside his messages. Sneaking the phone into the bathroom, she strolled through it for over an hour, as Derrick's snores increased her confidence that she had more than enough time to be on her creep shit.

It took a while, and some additional password solving, but before long she saw the person he was speaking to on the phone.

And her heart broke.

There were messages after messages of conversations with Flower, of an inappropriate nature. Not only did they have texts, but they also shared naked pictures and videos of her sticking River's dildo in her wet pussy.

No wonder he wanted to eat her pussy so much.

He was connecting with a fake lesbian.

But it was Derrick's dick photos for her. He sent them like they were memes. Like they weren't married. Like he wasn't somebody's husband.

Her heart ached.

It panged.

And she was certain that she would never recover.

But if she were to die, if she were to live no more, she was taking Derrick Louisville to the grave with her.

River and Flower were at the grocery store getting the ingredients for dinner later. They were picking up vegetables for the salad when suddenly Flower looked up at her and grinned.

"What you staring at me like that for, girl?"

"You take such good care of me," she smiled. "Why?"

River shrugged. "I don't know."

Flower dropped the tomato back in the bin in an effort to fake fight. "Why you say it like that?"

"You want me to be real with you?" She crossed her arms over her chest, as a few chicks looked at River and grinned, loving her style.

"Always."

"Everything in my spirit says you a snake."

Flower's stomach bubbled, not expecting her answer. "Wha...what?"

"I know it's harsh but it's the truth." She shrugged. "How else can you leave a person for a nigga when the only thing I ever did to you was support your dreams? And at the same time, I still took you back."

Flower swallowed the lump in her throat. "You scaring me."

River kissed her lips. "I don't mean for you to be scared, but I want you to know the truth. I want you to know how I feel. Because I never want it to be a question between us. You don't deserve me. But I'ma ride with you, shawty, in the hopes that you can be a better woman one day. And the day you don't become that and more…" she placed a fake gun against her head and said, "Boom…you're gone."

Flower smiled but she wanted to run. This brand of River was different. She aroused both fear and sexual desires in her at the same time. "I understand."

River winked and said, "So we shopping or —."

They both were put on pause when Banks strolled up to them like a cool breeze. He smelled good and was flanked by two men. Everything about him said money, power and respect.

"Banks," River said, raising her head high, as if challenging him.

"You followed me to the restaurant the other day. Why?"

"Who said I was following you? Mason was also there."

"What were you doing there?" Banks said firmer. "Because you have a problem with who you give your loyalty to, and that's going to cost you."

Flower, seeing a chance to look big and bad jumped in the conversation. "She's not scared of you! What are you anyway? Man? Female? A he she?" She laughed. "Girl, bye!"

No one, not even River found her comment amusing.

But what she did succeed in doing, is getting the wrong man's attention.

Banks removed his smokey shades and said, "I will remember you." With that he looked at her harder and walked away.

After following Banks to the grocery store, Mason's men, on his orders, were waiting on Banks to walk out so they could be done with him once and for all. Since it was six of them, and only two men protecting Banks, Mason felt confident that they would succeed in snatching him without error.

He gave one order.

Take him alive.

Mason, on the other hand, was a block away from the store, waiting on what he felt would be a success. Of course, he didn't want this drama with his old friend. But after the perceived hits on his head, he was ready for war.

The moment Banks walked out the store, the men charged, in an effort to snatch him, but there was one problem.

They didn't account for the two truckloads of men sitting outside of the store, waiting on the billionaire to come out. They didn't anticipate that per usual, Banks saw the set-up coming which meant he was prepared.

He always thought five steps ahead.

And so, the moment the men descended upon the trio, they were shot on spot.

Their bodies dropping like moths to flames.

People scampered away, screaming and yelling as Banks stood amongst the melee, without a care in the world.

Unharmed.

Unbothered.

And untouched.

He had to admit, that being around the gunfire, being around the chaos, was the third time since the memory loss that he felt like himself.

The first being when he cut his hair and started wearing masculine clothing.

The second being when he reunited with his adult children.

And the third, on the night his old friend tried to snatch him off the streets.

In the end the kidnapping attempt on Mason's part was a flop, and only succeeded in making things worse for the eldest Lou.

Mason was sitting in his car a block away calling everybody under the sun. Although it was bad business, he decided to leave a message on one of his hitmen's phone. Wanting everything to happen quickly, he was losing his cool which exposed his weaknesses.

With the burner phone pressed firmly against his cheek he said, "Look, I don't know what's going on, but somebody better tell me something! I been waiting all—."

Suddenly a bat came through the passenger side window and then the driver's side window. Glass shattered on his face and body as if he'd been in a major car accident.

Mason tried to throw the car in drive to get away, but his efforts proved unsuccessful when he was snatched out, thrown into a van and taken from the scene.

CHAPTER TWENTY-TWO

PETIT ESTATE

Spacey was sitting in the living room of the Petit Estate with Walid. Their relationship had only gotten better with time, and it was definitely something Spacey looked forward to during the week.

If only he could shake the eerie feeling off of being in the house. The same house that held him hostage in the attic for years.

They were playing video games when Walid asked, "Are you going to the island? To live with us in paradise?"

Spacey frowned, surprised he knew that much about adult business. "I don't know."

"I hope so."

He nodded. "I hope so too."

Suddenly Walid got quiet.

"What is it, little man?"

"I told you about that before. I'm not little."

Spacey laughed. "You right. I won't call you that again. Plus, the things you be doing for everybody, you definitely been on your grown man shit." He chuckled. "But what's up? Because you sounded sad on the phone when you called me over."

"I'm having dreams."

He frowned. "What kind of dreams?"

"Dreams about my brother."

Spacey nodded. "He'll be okay. You know that right?"

"I think he's ready to come home."

"How you figure?"

"He's changed. He's scared."

Spacey let the young man talk. He couldn't call a fake or foul because one thing about Walid was that he felt that the child had been on earth before.

He was wise beyond his years.

And so, if he said he felt Ace was ready to come home, maybe he was. Maybe he could feel the energy that only twins had access to.

"So, you think if he comes back, he won't be bad anymore?"

Walid looked at him, and with the voice of a man many times his age he said, "For now anyway."

Spacey nodded having respected the answer.

Besides, who could speak on the future if the past was still a factor?

They were about to play another round of video games when Spacey caught Carl from the corner of his eye. He was holding a plate and ascending the steps. Spacey never liked the man who helped keep him and Minnesota hostage in the attic, at Gina's request. But he decided to let bygones be bygones.

For now, anyway.

Still, for some reason he felt inclined to follow him up the stairs.

And that's exactly what he did.

Mason was at the lowest level of an industrial building Banks used to formulate his cosmetics.

Except this wasn't business.

Mason was tied up on a chair, with Banks standing in front of him and three men behind him.

"For somebody who doesn't remember the past, you sure are sliding into Banks' shoes with ease." Mason spit out blood, having been banged to the face many times that night.

"You tried to kill me. So, I'm protecting myself."

"Because you tried to kill me first!" He yelled, as he wiggled so hard it looked as if he would escape the ropes.

For his efforts, one of the three men who was protecting Banks, stole Mason in the face.

Mason settled down.

After ensuring he was restrained properly, Banks looked at his men. "You can leave us."

"Are you sure?" Goon One asked. "Because I don't trust him."

"I'm fine. I'll call you back if I need you."

They looked at Mason and walked away.

Banks grabbed a chair and sat directly in front of him.

It was tough thinking that at one time in life, Mason gave Banks his shoes because Banks' were holey. It was tough thinking that at one point the two would give their lives for one another.

And now, it was obvious that they would take the other's life in a heartbeat if given a chance.

"You started this, Banks." Mason spit out more blood. "And I'm not gonna lie, this shit here, is tearing me apart."

"All I wanted was for you to stay out of Ace and Walid's lives. To let us go about our business without fucking with us. And yet you couldn't even do that. You couldn't let go, even though you were never supposed to be involved in the first place."

"That doesn't matter."

"Fuck does that mean?"

"Yes, it's true. I wasn't supposed to be in their lives. But I met them, Banks and everything changed. I can't walk away."

"You can't walk away because you still want to have a connection with me, even after all of this."

Mason looked at him and thought about his response. He decided to be real. "I don't deny that."

Banks was shocked. "Why is it so important that you hold onto the past?" He was so angry he was trembling.

"Because I love you. Have always. Will always. And one day you will remember how much you care about me. I just hope it's not too late."

Banks jumped up and paced in front of his chair. "None of that shit matters anymore! It never mattered if you want to know the truth. How about it was all a lie. How about I never loved you, even when you tricked me into being who you wanted me to be. "

He squinted. "So, you're saying it was *all* a lie? None of the time we spent together was real? Because if you tell me that, then I don't give a fuck about shit anymore. And you can do whatever you want. Even take my life." He paused. "So, tell me, did you ever care about me? Fuck the past, I understand you don't remember the past. But what about when we lived together?"

Banks walked around a few seconds and then looked him dead in the eyes. "I never cared about you. Ever. Past or present. And I definitely don't care if you die today."

Mason sat back and it was as if the air had been pushed from his body. "Then you might as well take my life."

"I have plans for you that you don't even know about," Banks smiled. "Trust me I — ."

"Spacey was raped."

Banks frowned. "What you talking about?"

"Spacey was raped and I knew about it. And you might not give a fuck now, but the real Banks would have cared. A lot."

Upon hearing the news, Banks' mind was twirling and the emotions he felt were hard to decipher. For some reason, he was angry, but he couldn't understand why. Could it be that once again Mason was trying to control the situation and get Banks to kill him? Or was it because Banks, who was inside of the *new Banks'* soul, felt rage at what he learned about his oldest son?

"Who raped Spacey?"

"My son. Howard."

The moment Banks heard the name, he thought about the dream he had about someone killing Howard.

"Is that why you killed him? Because he raped my son?"

Mason's eyebrows rose. "What you talking about?"

"I had a dream of someone taking Howard's life. As real as I am standing here right now. And I always thought you were involved. Even tried to talk to you about Howard but you said you didn't know him. It wasn't until I went to Jersey that I realized he was real. And you were probably lying due to what you had done."

Mason's temples rocked.

Because in that moment, he was learning that Banks just may have been responsible for his son's death. In the past he thought Banks wanted to talk about Howard when he was Blaire, just because he remembered him, like he had many who were a part of his past.

Never, ever, did he think he remembered him because he was there the day he died.

"Tell me what you saw," Mason said, nostrils flaring.

"I saw enough to know you're foul."

"Tell me!" Mason roared.

"I saw Howard, in a motel. Like I was sitting on the bed, watching his last breath and..."

Suddenly the words were trapped in Banks' throat and he felt stupid. For it was at that moment, that he knew what he experienced was not due to Mason killing Howard. But possibly, because he killed Howard himself.

"You killed my son," Mason said through clenched teeth.

"I...I don't...I...why would I do that?"

"You must've found out he raped Spacey. But it could also be because he killed your ex-wife...Bet."

"But I—."

Suddenly Banks' cell phone rang.

Maybe it was because he was in need of a distraction, but he decided to answer. "Spacey, now is not a—."

"You have to come home!"

"I'll be there when I can. It's—."

"Pops! This is serious! Drop everything and get here! Now!"

When Banks rushed through the door of the Petit Estate, he was shocked to see the house flooded with officers and people he didn't recognize. Spacey was on the sofa, at Walid's side, as men in blue walked up and down his stairs.

Concerned, Banks rushed over to Spacey. "What's going on? Why is everybody in my fucking house?"

Spacey shook his head slowly, not wanting to talk in front of Walid. "I can't...tell you right..."

Banks yanked his arm and walked him away from the boy. "What is happening? Why are all of these people in my house?" He looked around.

"Carmen."

"What about her?"

"They found her. In your house."

He stumbled backwards. "What you talking about? Where was she?"

"In the attic. The butler put her there. In the same place as me and Minnesota spent a few years of our lives."

Banks' eyes widened. "Is she alive?"

Silence.

"Is she alive!"

Spacey looked in the direction the officers came and exited. "I don't know, Pops. They haven't told me anything yet. And, Pops, what is it about that attic? Why do you ignore it so much?"

He looked down. "I don't know, Spacey. I guess I'll never know."

At that moment, as if things couldn't get any worse, Ace's social worker walked through the door. She was in awe, like everyone else at the chaos.

Banks, spotting her, rushed over to her instantly. "Let's talk outside."

"What's going on, Mr. Wales?"

"Let's talk outside," when she didn't budge, he stepped closer. "Please."

River was sitting outside in her car in front of her apartment building, trying to reach Mason on the phone. When he didn't answer the first five calls, she was about to pull off to find him when Flower rushed out of the door wearing a pink robe.

She looked frantic. "Where are you going, baby?"

"I gotta peel out. Why, what's wrong? Why would you get on the elevator like that? You know how my neighbors are."

"But where are you going?"

"Why, Flower? I'm busy."

Fake tears streamed down her face. "I need some money. Like, a lot of money." She rubbed her arms like she was on drugs.

"Okay, take it from the stash in the house."

"I need more."

She frowned. "More than two hundred thousand stacks?"

"Yes. Five hundred thousand."

"What the fuck! Why?"

"Somebody kidnapped my father. They know I'm dating you, think I got some money and…and they snatched him off the streets."

River's heart thumped.

In that moment she could stay, get more information or leave and find her boss. Her next words would prove her loyalty.

"I'm sorry, babe, but now is a bad time. I'll help you through this I promise. Until then, I'll send my mans over here later. But I really gotta go now." She peeled out leaving her alone.

Irritated that she wasn't chosen, Flower pulled her phone from her pocket. "She isn't going for it right now. Fuck!" She said to her husband. "Something is up."

"I don't know what it is. We tried to do everything as planned. Maybe we should pull out with whatever cash we can get. Besides, Mason done killed my man behind that house and everything. I heard he said Banks sent him but still."

"Maybe we did our jobs. Maybe we just gotta wait to see what will happen next."

"Are you sure we shouldn't just take the two hundred thousand in her apartment and bounce?"

"Nah, I want more. I gotta have more. And I'ma get what's coming to me too."

Due to the cell phone tracker River had on Mason's phone, which she placed on when she was at his house one day, she had his location.

Easing out of her car, with her gun hanging closely against her body, and the cell phone in her hand, she moved toward the location where Mason was held.

When she happened upon a large industrial building for Strong Curls, she was stuck.

Did Banks steal Mason's phone?

She saw a few men who looked like guards on the side of the structure, and she shook them due to them playing dice, waiting on Banks to call them back into the building.

All of her questions were answered, when within five minutes of hunting, she found him tied up on a chair in the lowest part of the building.

"What the fuck!" She tucked her weapon in the back of her pants and quickly undid his ropes.

"How did you find me?" He asked.

"You gonna get mad," she continued as she freed him.

"Just tell me."

"I put a tracker on your phone." She pointed at his pocket. "Where is your cell?"

"He took it from me but it's probably in here somewhere." For a second he looked at her hard. Not because he was angry, but it was at that point that he realized how much she cared about him. He also realized something else. That he would never challenge her loyalty ever again.

"Where we going now?"

Rubbing his sore wrists, he said, "To the Petit Estate. I just found out Banks killed my son."

PETIT ESTATE

Filled with rage, Mason was on his way into the estate when he saw Jersey standing outside the property smoking a cigarette. As River stood guard, he walked up to her. Police were everywhere.

"What are you doing here?" She asked, blowing smoke into the air. "Banks will kill you if he sees you at his house. And what happened to your fucking face?" She dropped the cigarette and snuffed out the flames.

"What's going on inside?" Mason asked. "Why are all these cops here? Is Walid okay?"

"They found Carmen inside."

He stepped back. "What? Where?"

"In the attic. She's dead. Apparently while Preach was on the hunt for her, Carl knew her patterns, having been around the family forever. He somehow drugged her, got her here and kept her upstairs. She was raped and eventually took her own life."

"You gotta be fucking kidding me. This big bitch was always around my son and he out here raping people and shit!"

"Now what the fuck are you doing here? Because as you can see, it's a bad time."

He glared. "It's about Banks."

"What about him?"

Despite it all, he still hesitated on what he was about to say next. It could destroy everything.

"He killed our son. He killed Howard. That's why he was asking about him when he was Blaire."

Jersey's mouth hung open as all the air in her lungs escaped. "Don't fucking play with me."

"About this, I would never play. He killed him. The only question is, what do you want to do now?"

It was a long night that poured into the next day...

Unfortunately, the homicide investigation at the Petit Estate went into the morning. And for now, the war would have to stop between the old friends.

Because in the living room, on the sofa, sat Banks, Walid and Mason. They were hoping she would return the boy to them, although it looked bleak. With the social worker sitting in the recliner across from them, things seemed worse.

Looking at Mason's bruised face, the social worker took a deep breath. "What happened to you?"

Mason could've told the truth.

He could've said that Banks' men beat him to within every inch of his life. But instead, he said, "I fell on a bag of ice. Face first."

"What's going to happen with Ace?" Banks said, restoring the purpose of the meeting for the moment.

"I have to admit, after seeing what I saw last night, I'm not sure returning a child to this environment will be good."

"It's not our fault that my butler had a woman held in my attic." Banks said. "But I'll buy another house. It's done."

"So, who's fault is it, if it's not yours?"

"It's Carl's fault. And he's in police custody. Maybe we should leave it at that."

"It's not going to be that easy. He's — ."

"He's my brother!" Walid yelled while holding Mason's and Banks' hands as he sat between them. "And he's not supposed to be away this long. And...and you have to give my brother back. So, he can be better. Okay?"

The social worker looked at the boy who had Ace's entire face and sighed. "It's not as simple as it sounds, little man."

He glared, but like Carl had warned kept his cool even though she disrespected his stature. "I want my brother back."

"I know you do. But I promise you this, I will take into consideration what you've said here. I will take into consideration that you need him, as much as he needs you. That I can guarantee you."

The sky was a brilliant blue as Banks and the Wales family sat in a chartered jet flying over Baltimore City. What he was about to say, he wanted to make sure that only his family would hear.

In attendance were Spacey, Minnesota, Joey and Shay, and they were rattled upon hearing his next words.

Wearing brown ombre smoked colored shades, which complimented his black button-down shirt and black slacks, he was giving big dick energy for sure.

"I feel guided by Banks," he said as he gazed out of the window and into the clear blue skies. "This person, who you all love inspires my every move."

"Why you say that, Pops?" Joey asked.

"Because I feel as if I'm ready to blow up the world, and anybody in it who attempts to separate me from my family. Who attempts to separate me from you."

"Yep, that's Pops for sure," Spacey nodded.

Banks smiled before allowing it to disappear from his face. Besides, this meeting was serious.

"I'm concerned about Walid."

"What about Walid?" Minnesota asked, wiping her hair out of her face.

"I feel he may unravel if he isn't reunited with his brother. Now."

"I agree," Spacey nodded.

"And although I never had any intentions on letting him stay in that facility forever, I'm now giving them even less time to make a decision on their plans."

"What does that mean?" Shay asked, who hadn't gotten any sleep since she found out Derrick was cheating on her with Flower.

He looked outside again. "As Blaire, I was a lawful person. I believed in doing things by the book, because in my opinion, making moves based on rules and regulations was right." He sighed deeply. "But these people are fucking with my son. And I won't let that happen for much longer."

Spacey rubbed his hands together. "What do you need from us?"

"I'll give you the details on my plans soon but in the meantime, I need you all to make a decision. Because when I pull Ace out of that place, legally or by violence, we won't be here the next day to see the fallout. We will be in Belize. We will be on our island."

They all looked at one another.

"I need to know if you're with me. I need to know if we are together. And I need to know if you stand by what it means to be called a Wales. Because I'm willing to die and kill for my name. The question is, are you?"

EPILOGUE

THE PRECINCT

The Butler sat in the interrogation room, as the detectives were propped at the table across from him.

"What you're saying doesn't make sense," Detective One said.

Carl tried to get comfortable in the small seat, but he was so large his legs didn't fall the right way and as a result, caused his lower back to hurt. "I don't know what you want from me."

"You claim she had got a hold of young Ace and convinced him to be violent."

"She did. As a matter of fact, when I found her at her best friend's house, a woman she used to do drugs with for a while, she said getting at Ace was her way of

Truce 3: Sins of The Fathers

getting back at her mother. And also, Banks, for taking her place in Gina's life."

"But wasn't Gina rich? How did she survive without getting paid?"

"Her brother Hercules was giving her money. He pretended not to know where she was located, but he knew everything. All I wanted, was to keep her away from the twins."

"Is that why you raped her?"

He smiled. "She was still attractive, even in her older age. Why not fuck her if I could?"

The detectives looked at one another in disgust. "I can't see putting everything on the line for a kid. Seems weird at best."

"She was responsible for a lot of pain and anxiety for the boy. Especially Walid. And he's my guy. And I just wanted to make things better."

"Is that why you fed her and had sex with her even after she died?"

"Like I said, why should good pussy go to waste?" He sat back. "Now are we done? Because I am."

"No. Tell us everything about the Petits, Wales and Louisville's. Everything you know."

Flower was in River's arms as they lie in bed. When she opened her eyes, she stole a second to take in each feature of River's face. The woman was cool, no doubt, and she realized even more why she was attracted to her in the first place.

If only her heart wasn't tied up with her husband, maybe they could've had a second chance at love.

A real chance.

When River opened her lids and saw her looking up at her, wiping her eyes, she said, "What you looking at girl?"

"Thank you again for the money to get my father back." She grinned.

River shrugged. "It's nothing. I just hope it helps."

"He's home." She said excitedly. "I just got off the phone with my sister. I didn't want to wake you so I let you sleep."

"Word?" River smiled while looking at her cell phone.

"I really do thank you, River. For everything you did for me. I know five hundred thousand dollars is a little money for you, but it saved my father."

"Anything for you, kid." She kissed her on the forehead and eased out of bed. She then looked at her phone. "Let me piss right quick though. I be back." She winked.

The moment she left, Flower stole another second to take in the scenery, knowing that when it was all said and done, she would be leaving again.

Forever.

When she eased off the bed to grab her robe, she heard someone enter the room. "I'm about to make breakfast for you now."

"Sit down."

When she heard the voice of someone other than River, she almost died on site.

Turning around slowly, she was face to face with Banks Wales. He had two men on his side. And none of them looked happy to see her snake ass.

"Please don't hurt me." She said easing out of bed.

"Sit down."

She was trembling too much to comply.

Calmly, but firmly, he said, "Now…"

Slowly she eased on the edge of the bed and almost slipped off like wet shit.

"Your husband is dead. Mason went over there earlier in the day and took care of him. But before he died, he told us everything. The plotting. The planning. And after putting one and one together, and talking to

River, we got everything we needed from him. Even River's money back."

She shook her head slowly from left to right. "Please don't hurt me."

Banks walked further into the room. "I gotta know, what was the point in all of this?"

"I just...I just..."

"You know what, it doesn't matter. It won't change a thing. You got in the middle of a major situation. Caused a lot of powerful people harm and now it's over. Do you have anything you want to say? Anything that will make things better for anybody left who gives a fuck about you?"

"No..." she said shaking her head faster. "But please don't do this."

He smiled. "Somebody wants to talk to you."

He walked out, leaving two of his men behind as River walked inside.

Flower jumped up and rushed toward her. Dropping to her knees she said, "Okay, okay, listen, we can make this work." She wiped her tears away, and smiled, believing she could talk her way out of shit per usual.

"Word?" River folded her arms. "I'm listening."

"Yes, we can, see, we can go away. We can get married and…and have some kids of our own. That way, that way we can prove that two women can be together and make a family. We can prove to the world that we deserve to be happy, just like any other couple."

River nodded. "You know, it wasn't until this moment that I got why you really left."

Her eyes widened. "What do you mean?"

"You were ashamed of our relationship. You were ashamed of us."

"No, I, I mean, I was just, you know, because when you met me, I was straight. But I fell in love. And now I realize we deserve each other and — ."

She was disgusted. "Bitch, I told you, you don't deserve me. Never have. Never will."

"River, just let me go—."

"But I'ma ride with you, shawty, in the hopes that you can be a better woman one day." River said, reciting what she had said to her when they were in the grocery store.

She sniffled and wiped her tears. "What?"

"And the day you don't become that and more..." River removed a weapon from the back of her pants and placed it against her head. *"Boom..."*

She fired, splattering brain matter everywhere.

"You're gone."

PETIT ESTATE

It was a magnificent day...

Blue skies…

And a vibrant yellow sun.

Mason and Jersey were on the veranda of the Petite Estate, waiting for Banks to return.

Earlier that afternoon, Banks called them all together to put on pause the drama, until they could get Ace out of Children's Hospital. Besides, after it was later discovered that Flower originated all the chaos, they thought they could simmer a bit.

At least until Ace returned.

But Jersey seemed different, after hearing the news about Howard. And Mason was concerned that once again he shared information with someone who was not able to put away their emotions so easily as he and Banks had become accustomed to doing.

"Listen, I need you to keep what you learned to yourself for now," Mason said. "Let's get Ace out of the place, and then we can discuss what happened with Howard later."

She stared at him blankly.

"Jersey, do you hear me?"

Silence.

Mason stepped closer. "Listen, don't do nothing stupid right now. We can handle things later, but let's get Ace back and—."

Banks entered the veranda. "Okay, I think they're going to set up another meeting with us about Ace. If we go in the hospital calm, and show we can work together, Dr. Porter may release him to us tonight. That way—."

"All I wanna know, is if it's true," Jersey said looking directly at Banks.

Mason sighed and shook his head.

"Is what true?" Banks replied, gazing at her.

"Did you kill my son?" Jersey looked at him directly in the eyes. "Did you kill Howard? My boy?"

Banks looked down and shook his head. "Jersey, I don't know. I have been more honest with you about this period in my life than anybody. I told you what I remember and what I don't. And all I can say is, if I go on my dreams, I was there. It doesn't mean I killed him though."

"He's right, Jersey," Mason cosigned.

With that Jersey pulled out a gun and aimed at him. "You had me in your bed while you murdered my son? Is that what you're telling me?"

"Jersey, put it down!" Mason pleaded. "You heard him say he can't remember."

"Well maybe I should shoot you instead!" She said aiming at Mason now. "Since all you fuckers seem to care about is each other. While dragging the rest of us in this for your amusement! For your fun."

"Jersey, please don't do this," Banks said. "I'm begging you not to make any move before you — ."

She squeezed.

And Mason saw it first.

On impulse, he jumped in front of Banks, covering his body with his own.

For his efforts, a bullet entered his back and spine.

Jersey, having hit the wrong person, dropped the gun. With the father of her children going down, she quickly returned to reason.

"No, no, no!" She grabbed her face.

Spacey who was in the house and heard the melee rushed out. "What's going on?!"

"Son, call 911!" Banks directed as he held Mason in his arms. "Now!"

As Mason grew weak, he focused on the beautiful clear sky. For some reason it brought him great calm.

Banks, at the same time was a wreck. As blood from Mason's body poured into Banks' hands, suddenly memories of the past came flooding back.

Memories of it all.

Of their lives together when they were kids.

Of the good and bad times.

And Banks was crushed.

That he was watching his closest friend, the man who meant the world to him, close his eyes.

COMING SOON

TRUCE 4

THE FINALE

Truce 3: Sins of The Fathers

CARTEL PUBLICATIONS

PRESENTS

The Cartel Publications Order Form

www.thecartelpublications.com

Inmates **ONLY** receive novels for $10.00 per book **PLUS** shipping fee **PER BOOK.**
(Mail Order **MUST** come from inmate directly to receive discount)

Shyt List 1	_____	$15.00
Shyt List 2	_____	$15.00
Shyt List 3	_____	$15.00
Shyt List 4	_____	$15.00
Shyt List 5	_____	$15.00
Shyt List 6	_____	$15.00
Pitbulls In A Skirt	_____	$15.00
Pitbulls In A Skirt 2	_____	$15.00
Pitbulls In A Skirt 3	_____	$15.00
Pitbulls In A Skirt 4	_____	$15.00
Pitbulls In A Skirt 5	_____	$15.00
Victoria's Secret	_____	$15.00
Poison 1	_____	$15.00
Poison 2	_____	$15.00
Hell Razor Honeys	_____	$15.00
Hell Razor Honeys 2	_____	$15.00
A Hustler's Son	_____	$15.00
A Hustler's Son 2	_____	$15.00
Black and Ugly	_____	$15.00
Black and Ugly As Ever	_____	$15.00
Ms Wayne & The Queens of DC **(LGBT)**	_____	$15.00
Black And The Ugliest	_____	$15.00
Year Of The Crackmom	_____	$15.00
Deadheads	_____	$15.00
The Face That Launched A Thousand Bullets	_____	$15.00
The Unusual Suspects	_____	$15.00
Paid In Blood	_____	$15.00
Raunchy	_____	$15.00
Raunchy 2	_____	$15.00
Raunchy 3	_____	$15.00
Mad Maxxx (4th Book Raunchy Series)	_____	$15.00
Quita's Dayscare Center	_____	$15.00
Quita's Dayscare Center 2	_____	$15.00
Pretty Kings	_____	$15.00
Pretty Kings 2	_____	$15.00
Pretty Kings 3	_____	$15.00
Pretty Kings 4	_____	$15.00
Silence Of The Nine	_____	$15.00
Silence Of The Nine 2	_____	$15.00
Silence Of The Nine 3	_____	$15.00

By T. STYLES

Prison Throne	_____	$15.00
Drunk & Hot Girls	_____	$15.00
Hersband Material **(LGBT)**	_____	$15.00
The End: How To Write A	_____	$15.00
Bestselling Novel In 30 Days (Non-Fiction Guide)		
Upscale Kittens	_____	$15.00
Wake & Bake Boys	_____	$15.00
Young & Dumb	_____	$15.00
Young & Dumb 2: Vyce's Getback	_____	$15.00
Tranny 911 **(LGBT)**	_____	$15.00
Tranny 911: Dixie's Rise **(LGBT)**	_____	$15.00
First Comes Love, Then Comes Murder	_____	$15.00
Luxury Tax	_____	$15.00
The Lying King	_____	$15.00
Crazy Kind Of Love	_____	$15.00
Goon	_____	$15.00
And They Call Me God	_____	$15.00
The Ungrateful Bastards	_____	$15.00
Lipstick Dom **(LGBT)**	_____	$15.00
A School of Dolls **(LGBT)**	_____	$15.00
Hoetic Justice	_____	$15.00
KALI: Raunchy Relived	_____	$15.00
(5th Book in Raunchy Series)		
Skeezers	_____	$15.00
Skeezers 2	_____	$15.00
You Kissed Me, Now I Own You	_____	$15.00
Nefarious	_____	$15.00
Redbone 3: The Rise of The Fold	_____	$15.00
The Fold (4th Redbone Book)	_____	$15.00
Clown Niggas	_____	$15.00
The One You Shouldn't Trust	_____	$15.00
The WHORE The Wind		
Blew My Way	_____	$15.00
She Brings The Worst Kind	_____	$15.00
The House That Crack Built	_____	$15.00
The House That Crack Built 2	_____	$15.00
The House That Crack Built 3	_____	$15.00
The House That Crack Built 4	_____	$15.00
Level Up **(LGBT)**	_____	$15.00
Villains: It's Savage Season	_____	$15.00
Gay For My Bae	_____	$15.00
War	_____	$15.00
War 2: All Hell Breaks Loose	_____	$15.00
War 3: The Land Of The Lou's	_____	$15.00
War 4: Skull Island	_____	$15.00
War 5: Karma	_____	$15.00
War 6: Envy	_____	$15.00
War 7: Pink Cotton	_____	$15.00
Madjesty vs. Jayden (Novella)	_____	$8.99
You Left Me No Choice	_____	$15.00
Truce – A War Saga	_____	$15.00
Ask The Streets For Mercy	_____	$15.00
Truce 2 - The War of The Lou's	_____	$15.00
An Ace and Walid Very, Very Bad Christmas	_____	$15.00
Truce 3 – The Sins of The Fathers	_____	$15.00

Truce 3: Sins of The Fathers

(**Redbone 1** & **2** are **NOT** Cartel Publications novels and if **ordered** the cost is **FULL** price of $15.00 **each. No Exceptions**.)

Please add **$5.00** for shipping and handling fees for up to **(2) BOOKS PER ORDER**. (INMATES INCLUDED) (See next page for details)

The Cartel Publications * P.O. BOX 486 OWINGS MILLS MD 21117

Name: _____

Address: _____

City/State: _____

Contact/Email: _____

Please allow 10-15 BUSINESS days Before shipping.

PLEASE NOTE DUE TO **COVID-19** SOME ORDERS MAY TAKE UP TO **3 WEEKS OR LONGER** BEFORE THEY SHIP

*The Cartel Publications is **NOT** responsible for **Prison Orders** rejected!*

NO RETURNS and NO REFUNDS
NO PERSONAL CHECKS ACCEPTED
STAMPS NO LONGER ACCEPTED

By T. STYLES

CPSIA information can be obtained
at www.ICGtesting.com
Printed in the USA
LVHW031527040321
680607LV00002B/222